TRASHED!

TRASHED!

MARTHA FREEMAN

A Paula Wiseman Book

Simon & Schuster Books for Young Readers
NEW YORK LONDON TORONTO SYDNEY NEW DELHI

SIMON & SCHUSTER BOOKS FOR YOUNG READERS
An imprint of Simon & Schuster Children's Publishing Division
1230 Avenue of the Americas, New York, New York 10020

This book is a work of fiction. Any references to historical events, real people, or real places are used fictitiously. Other names, characters, places, and events are products of the author's imagination, and any resemblance to actual events or places or persons, living or dead, is entirely coincidental.

SIMON & SCHUSTER BOOKS FOR YOUNG READERS
and related marks are trademarks of Simon & Schuster, Inc.
For information about special discounts for bulk purchases,
please contact Simon & Schuster Special Sales at 1-866-506-1949 or
business@simonandschuster.com.
The Simon & Schuster Speakers Bureau can bring authors to your
live event. For more information or to book an event, contact
the Simon & Schuster Speakers Bureau at 1-866-248-3049 or
visit our website at www.simonspeakers.com.
Interior design by Hilary Zarycky
The text for this book was set in Life LT Std.
Manufactured in the United States of America
1222 FFG
First Edition
2 4 6 8 10 9 7 5 3 1
Library of Congress Cataloging-in-Publication Data
Names: Freeman, Martha, 1956– author.
Title: Trashed! / Martha Freeman.
Description: New York : Simon & Schuster Books for Young Readers, [2023] |
"A Paula Wiseman Book." | Audience: Ages 8–12. | Audience: Grades 4–6. |
Summary: After Arthur finds a chipped teacup on a shelf at his family's store,
he embarks on an adventure involving stolen jewels, a treacherous friendship,
prairie dogs, and even the ghost of a pet mouse.
Identifiers: LCCN 2022007389 (print) | LCCN 2022007390 (ebook) |
ISBN 9781665905350 (hardcover) | ISBN 9781665905374 (ebook)
Subjects: CYAC: Adventure and adventurers—Fiction. | Courage—Fiction. |
Friendship—Fiction. | Lost and found possessions—Fiction. | LCGFT: Novels.
Classification: LCC PZ7.F87496 Tp 2023 (print) | LCC PZ7.F87496 (ebook) |
DDC [Fic]—dc23
LC record available at https://lccn.loc.gov/2022007389
LC ebook record available at https://lccn.loc.gov/2022007390

For the Pearsall-Christman family:
Zach, Hamil, Arthur, and Simon—best neighbors ever

TRASHED!

CHAPTER ONE

Ramona's mouse died suddenly.

Friday night it had been scrabbling around the sawdust in its cage, whiskers twitching, eyes bright.

Saturday morning it was paws-up, eyes shut.

"Rigor mortis," said Arthur. He had heard those words in a movie and wanted to test them out.

"Okay, and it's a girl, and why did she die?" Ramona Popper was six. She didn't know what "rigor mortis" meant, but she would never ask her brother. She figured he was showing off, which he was.

Arthur Popper was eleven. He and his sister mostly ignored each other. But Ramona had gone to him when she'd found her mouse. Now they were standing in Ramona's bedroom, which was in the back of the family's apartment. Through the window was a view of hills, the Front Range of the Rocky Mountains. Arthur's room was on the other side and looked out on the street, cars going by.

"Do you know if the mouse was old?" Arthur asked.

Ramona wiped her nose with the back of her hand and sniffled. They were standing by the mouse's cage, which rested on a table by the window. The mouse didn't look peaceful exactly. The poor thing looked uncomfortable.

Ramona and Arthur were still wearing their pajamas, Ramona's blue with tiny red triangle trees, Arthur's red with a big green Grinch on the shirt—Christmas pajamas in April. Like a lot of Arthur's and Ramona's clothes, the pajamas had come from the store, which always had a good supply of kids' Christmas pajamas—worn once, outgrown by the next year.

Ramona didn't know if her mouse had been old.

Arthur could think of things besides old age that might kill a mouse. Things like germs and viruses and cancer. But Ramona was only in first grade. She didn't need to hear such bad stuff yet.

Arthur was not the best big brother, but he wasn't totally heartless.

"Should we bury her?" Ramona asked.

"Yes," Arthur said. "For a fact, I think we should have a funeral."

Ramona widened her eyes. "I've never been to a funeral before," she said.

Arthur hadn't either, but he'd seen them in movies. Organizing a funeral couldn't be that hard. Besides, Ramona wouldn't know if he got it wrong.

"The service will be at one o'clock," he announced. "After breakfast you can find a coffin—a box to bury the mouse in."

"I know what a coffin is, Arthur," Ramona said.

Arthur didn't have to say where Ramona would find a coffin. They both knew there would be a box in the store. That was a good thing about having the store downstairs. When you needed something, you could usually find it.

Arthur and Ramona ate cereal for breakfast at the big table in the kitchen. Even though it was Saturday, their mom, a lawyer, had gone to work to catch up. She had to do that a lot. Arthur pictured being a lawyer as one big race, with their mom a few steps behind.

As for Dad, the store didn't open till ten, but some rich Boulder citizen had died the week before, and Dad was downstairs sorting possessions the man's family didn't want. The next day, Sunday, Arthur and his best friend, Veda Lopez, would probably be assigned to help.

After she ate, Ramona went downstairs to find something she could use for a mouse coffin, and Arthur went back to his bedroom, where the cars outside—*swoosh, swoosh, swoosh*—made a soothing soundtrack.

CHAPTER TWO

The Popper family's apartment was the same size as the store below, big for only four people. Mom had a room that she called her library, and Dad had a room for old guitars. There was a formal dining room they never used, and a living room used at Christmastime for the tree.

In Arthur's room were a four-poster bed; a heavy wooden desk; two tall, mismatched bookcases; and a fat blue chair. Everything was from the store. Except for groceries, Arthur's family rarely shopped anywhere else.

Now Arthur threw his pajamas onto the floor, pulled on shorts and a Broncos T-shirt, and sat down at his computer. Online he learned that some people thought the purpose of a funeral was to help "the survivors" get over their sadness, while others thought it was to help "the soul of the deceased" move on from this life to whatever was next.

Does a mouse have a soul? Arthur wondered, but he

put the question away for later. Right now he had a funeral to plan.

What did you do at a funeral anyway? The websites said you should pray and say nice things about the deceased, but some funerals had parades and even dancing!

Arthur went to find Ramona. By this time she was back in her own room, sitting on the floor, decorating a small box using markers, paint, and glitter.

She held the box up with her fingertips, trying not to smudge everything. "Do you think it's too gaudy?" she asked.

Arthur thought she must be trying out a new word too. "Was she a gaudy kind of mouse?" he asked.

Ramona thought for a second. "I guess," she said.

"So that's good, then," Arthur said. "And what kind of music did she like?"

Ramona's face was thin-lipped and serious, her dark eyebrows as bushy as caterpillars. *"Frozen,"* she said finally.

Arthur wrote this down. "After the coffin is ready," he said, "you should wrap up the body in a napkin or something, and then put it in."

"Okay," Ramona said.

"Will it creep you out to touch her?"

"I'll wash my hands after," Ramona said.

Arthur nodded. "One more thing. What was her name?"

Ramona blinked. "You don't know?"

"I'm sorry," Arthur said. "I won't forget after today."

"Mouse 4," Ramona said.

Arthur's bangs were long, so when his eyebrows rose, Ramona couldn't see. "Seriously?"

Ramona looked down at the box. "I know it's a bad name, but it's what the pet store called her, and I was going to give her a better one, but there are so many names you can name a mouse. And then I got used to 'Mouse 4.'"

Arthur thought it would be mean to criticize at a time like this. So instead he asked other questions. What activities did Mouse 4 enjoy? Was she generous? Did she have a big heart? He had looked online at obituaries and noticed these things were often said. Sometimes the dead person had been well known for telling jokes and stories, but Mouse 4 couldn't talk, so Arthur didn't ask about that.

At a few minutes before one, Arthur went outside to a spot where he and his grandmother had recently planted flowers—petunias, alyssum, lobelia. The ground was soft; it took only a few minutes to dig the grave.

CHAPTER THREE

At one o'clock exactly Ramona met Arthur by the store's back door, and the funeral began. First came the procession, with Ramona going first, carrying Mouse 4 in the gaudy, slightly smudged coffin. The summer before, Ramona had been a flower girl at a cousin's wedding, and now she did the flower-girl walk—right foot, step together, left foot, step together. Arthur hadn't told her to do this. She had thought of it on her own.

Arthur was carrying four cookies on a plate and Ramona's iPad, which was playing "Let It Go." The cookies were the special-occasion ones that his parents kept on a high kitchen shelf. A funeral, Arthur decided, was a special occasion.

It was late April, the sun bright and warm, the sky blue except for some white clouds that looked painted on.

At flower-girl pace, it took a while to get to the grave

site. That seemed right to Arthur. You shouldn't hurry a funeral. When at last they arrived, Arthur turned off the music, Ramona placed the coffin into the hole, and they looked down at the mouse, wrapped in a piece of shiny rainbow-printed cloth.

"Should I put the lid on?" Ramona asked.

"Not yet," Arthur said. "First I have to talk."

Ramona said, "Okay." She looked like she was enjoying herself.

"Dearly beloved," Arthur began, using words he had gotten from a YouTube clip. "We are gathered here today to say goodbye to Mouse 4 and to wish her a happy life in heaven, or wherever nice place her soul is going."

(Arthur still hadn't decided whether rodents had souls, but he thought these words would comfort the survivor.)

"Mouse 4 was a good mouse," Arthur continued. "She enjoyed running on her wheel and eating her pellets. She looked cute when she wiggled her whiskers, and she had a very pink tail. Mouse 4 didn't mind when Ramona took her out of her cage and petted her. She only ran away a couple of times, and she always ran under the same dresser, so she was easy to find."

"She got kind of dusty, though," Ramona added.

"Did she mean to get dusty?" Arthur asked.

"I don't think so," Ramona said.

"So that's okay, then," Arthur said. "Mouse 4 was kind and generous, we think. She may have known jokes and stories, but she didn't share them. Would you like to say a few words, Ramona?"

Ramona looked down at the coffin she had decorated. It had turned out pretty well, and she was feeling bad that it was about to be covered in dirt. But she wasn't going to say so. "Mouse 4 was my best mouse," she said. "Goodbye, Mouse 4."

"Ashes to ashes, and dust to dust," Arthur said, which had been on the YouTube clip too. "Amen. Now you say 'Amen' too, Ramona."

Ramona did.

"And now you put the lid on the box."

Ramona did. The lid had pink glitter-glue stripes and flower stickers. In the middle was a large cutout letter *M*.

"You're going to put dirt on it, aren't you?" Ramona said.

"Yes," Arthur said.

Ramona took a breath and let it out. "Okay."

"You can make a cross or something to mark the grave

too," Arthur pointed out. "Like with Popsicle sticks? Or you could decorate a rock. That won't get buried."

"Maybe I will," Ramona said. "Is it time for cookies?"

Until that day, Arthur had never thought much about Ramona's mouse. He had probably only held it a couple of times, felt the four little prickle paws tickling his palm, admired the long pink hairless tail. Ramona had touched the mouse's nose to hers sometimes. Arthur had seen her. Arthur had never done anything like that. The mouse was a rodent. How cozy did a person want to be with a rodent?

After the funeral, Arthur thought he was done forever with Mouse 4.

Which is why he was so surprised when, late that same night, he realized Mouse 4 was haunting him.

CHAPTER FOUR

The family store was called Universal Trash, established by Byron and Linda Baer in 1980. Byron and Linda Baer were Arthur and Ramona's grandparents, their mother's parents. In the beginning the store had been a small place located next to a convenience store in a strip mall on Valmont Road, its secondhand merchandise laid out on folding tables. The store never sold anything that wasn't clean, and if there were multiple pieces, like for a blender or a vacuum cleaner, all the pieces were there, nothing chipped or cracked.

The store became popular quickly and moved to its current much larger location, a renovated warehouse on Broadway in North Boulder. At first the second floor of the building was storage space. Later, when houses in Boulder got crazy-expensive, it was remodeled into an apartment for Arthur's mom and her family.

Arthur's grandparents had never bothered with advertising. Arthur's grandfather, who did not like to spend money, had called advertising a needless expense. But when Arthur's dad had taken over, he'd had his own ideas, and one had been a slogan, "Trashy is classy!" that had appeared in ads in the local newspaper, on signs at the store, sometimes even on banners on the sides of buses. Now that slogan was a decade old, and Dad had been thinking about an update with an environmental theme.

At dinner one night about a month before Mouse 4 died, the family brainstormed ideas.

"The problem," Ramona announced after a while, "is that nothing rhymes with 'earth.'"

"'Dearth,'" Arthur said.

"That is not a word," Ramona said.

"Yeah, it is," Arthur said.

"If it's a word, what does it mean?" Ramona scrunched her caterpillar brows.

"No idea," Arthur said.

"It means, uh . . . like 'lack.' Like 'not enough,'" Dad said. "'There's a dearth of money in my piggy bank.'"

Ramona stopped chewing and looked at her dad. "I didn't know you had a piggy bank."

"Neither did I," Mom said.

"I don't. It was an *example*," Dad said. "Like—there's a dearth of air in the football. There's a dearth of spaghetti on my plate. There's a dearth of—"

"—brains in Arthur's brain!" Ramona piped up.

"That's not funny," Arthur said. "And it doesn't even make sense."

Ordinarily Mom would have told them to simmer down, but she seemed to be busy thinking. At last she said, "How about this? 'Shop the Universe, don't trash it!'"

Dad said, "Too confusing. No one's talking about the environment of the whole *universe,* dear, only the environment of one *planet.*"

Mom sniffed and wiped her mouth. "Fine," she said. "I guess I should stick to law."

"I thought it was good, Mom," Arthur said.

"Thank you," Mom said.

Dad set down his fork. "Actually, I have an idea too: 'Sustain the earth, sustain your cash, shop at Universal Trash!'"

"Too confusing," Mom said.

"I like it," Arthur said.

"What does 'sustain' even mean?" Ramona asked.

"'Save,' more or less," Mom said.

"Say 'save,' then," Ramona said.

Arthur wasn't paying that much attention, but Mom and Dad were. They stopped chewing, looked at each other, looked at Ramona.

"You're a genius," Dad told her.

Ramona smiled one of her rare smiles. "I know."

"Save the earth and save your cash . . . ," Dad said, and then Mom and even Arthur—who had swallowed by this time—chimed in: "Shop at Universal Trash!"

All those years, Grandpa was wrong about advertising. It works. From the moment the new slogan showed up in the windows, on the website, and in the newspaper, all kinds of new customers began coming in, and the store got busier and busier.

CHAPTER FIVE

Arthur Popper was good at planning funerals but not at basketball.

Good at spelling but shaky on ice skates.

Good at customer service—talking to people in the store and being helpful—but not brave. Not at all.

So when Mouse 4's ghost appeared, Arthur was startled, scared almost. Nothing like this had ever happened to him.

"Good evening, Arthur," the mouse said in a small, pleasant voice, "and thank you for the funeral, even if the coffin was gaudy. You'd be surprised how many mice die and don't get a funeral at all."

Arthur sat up fast and tugged the covers to his neck. The speaker was sitting on her haunches on the bedpost nearest Arthur's right foot. She was more transparent than she had been in life and more luminous, but otherwise she looked the same. "Y-y-you're welcome?" Arthur said, blinking. To his embarrassment, his own voice squeaked.

"Your room is nice," Mouse 4 said, looking around. "I don't think I was ever in it before."

Arthur took a breath to slow his heart. "Thank you," he said, and then, "What are you doing here?"

"I'm not sure myself," Mouse 4 said. "I'm here to be helpful in some way, I expect."

"Do I need help?" Arthur asked.

"We all need help, Arthur," Mouse 4 said. "Even heroes and smart kids."

Arthur thought this was probably true.

"Anyway, don't mind me," Mouse 4 continued. "Feel free to go on back to sleep. Good night."

Arthur didn't think he'd be able to sleep but settled into his pillow. "Mouse 4?" he said, eyes closed.

"Yes?" the pleasant voice responded.

"Are you . . . uh? I mean, do you . . ."

"Spit it out, Arthur."

"Do you really like your name?"

Mouse 4's laugh was less a squeak than a chitter. "Not especially."

Arthur opened his eyes again, saw the mouse still perched on the bedpost. "If you're going to be around for a while, would you mind if I called you 'Watson'?"

Mouse 4 flicked her tail. "After Sherlock Holmes's friend?"

"You know about Sherlock Holmes?" Arthur said.

"Mice pay attention," Mouse 4 said. "It's a survival strategy."

Arthur said, "That makes sense. And yes. Sherlock Holmes is who I was thinking of. Watson helped him, after all. And I like detective stories. If you want, though, since you're a girl, we could change it to 'Wanda' or something."

Mouse 4 considered. "I think 'Watson' will do."

Arthur smiled. "Good night, Watson. See you tomorrow."

"Good night, Arthur," Watson said.

To Arthur's surprise, he fell right to sleep. And if Watson made noise scrabbling around the room, inspecting stuff, getting dusty, Arthur never even heard.

CHAPTER SIX

Watson wasn't around when Arthur woke up, and Arthur thought maybe he'd dreamed the whole thing.

He got dressed—same Broncos T-shirt and shorts—went into the bathroom, splashed water onto his face, looked at himself in the mirror. Grandpa B liked to say the family was Colorado royalty because his great-great-great-(Arthur wasn't sure how many greats)-grandfather, also named Arthur, had come to the territory before the Civil War, made a fortune mining silver, lost the fortune, then made another one raising sheep.

Arthur often tried to imagine what his ancestor's life had been like. He had left everybody and everything he knew; slept on hard ground; felt hunger; worked hard from sunup to sundown, maybe longer, not knowing if he'd ever have any money.

Also no computer, no car, no toilet even.

Arthur pushed the bangs back from his eyes, stared at his own reflection, tried to see some trace of his great-great-great. Was he there in the pale skin, the green eyes, the straight dark-blond hair? Maybe he was in the round cheeks, but his dad claimed the cheeks were from his side of the family, the Popper side. There was no royalty on the Popper side, just a lot of plain working people.

"What's on the agenda for today, Arthur?" Watson had appeared beside the hot-water tap. In daylight she looked even more transparent than she had in the dark. Until she spoke up, Arthur hadn't noticed her at all.

Arthur grinned, glad she was back, glad she hadn't been a dream. "Veda's coming over," he said. "She's my friend. On Sunday afternoons we both help out in the store." Arthur turned off the tap. "Uh . . . I'm gonna go eat breakfast now. How does this work exactly? If you want to come with me, do I pick you up? *Can* I pick you up?"

"No, no." Watson had been nosing around the tooth-brushes. Now she curled her tail and shrank back. "I am incorporeal, Arthur. Try to pick me up, and you'll grab nothing at all. But I'll see you later. You can count on that."

Arthur had recently learned that word, "incorporeal." It meant "without a body."

"Okay." He started for the door, then stopped. "Can I tell people about you?"

"Up to you," the mouse said. "You might want to think twice, though. Some people will think you're crazy."

Arthur didn't see Watson again that morning. He didn't tell Ramona about her either. He wasn't worried Ramona would think he was crazy. He didn't care about that. It was more he worried she might feel bad Mouse 4 wasn't haunting her.

The stairs from the family's apartment to the store led down from a landing by the pantry behind the kitchen. The landing itself served as the family's mudroom. There were hooks for coats, backpacks, and umbrellas, two low shelves for boots. On the wall were some old family photographs of Colorado long ago, the black-and-white kind that had gone yellow with age.

A few minutes before one o'clock, Arthur descended without turning on the light. At the bottom were two doors. One led outside to the parking lot. The other, which Arthur opened, led into the store's office. In the room were three old-fashioned wood desks, assorted chairs— comfortable and not—and a love seat. The walls were lined with shelves. Neatly arranged on the shelves were dozens and dozens of three-by-five index-card boxes.

Nothing matched—not the desks, the chairs, or even the index-card boxes.

Veda, always early, was seated behind one of the desks. Grandpa B was behind another, which meant Arthur's dad must have been out front helping customers.

"Here's the boy at last," said Grandpa B.

"I'm not late," Arthur said. "Am I?"

"Early bird catches the worm, Arthur," Grandpa said.

"If you like worms," Arthur said. "Hi, Veda."

"Hi back," Veda said. "We're supposed to inventory the costume jewelry from the Carson estate, your dad says. Maybe we'll find some diamonds and my mom can retire."

"And buy a castle!" Arthur said.

Veda shook her head. "She doesn't want a castle. Too much to dust."

"This girl's practical, Arthur," Grandpa B said. "If I were you, I'd propose now. She won't be on the market long."

Grandpa said embarrassing stuff like that a lot. Luckily, Veda was used to him.

"I don't want him," she said. "Too skinny."

Veda herself was strong, not skinny, with straight black hair and tawny skin.

"He'll fill out in time." Grandpa B gave Arthur a hard look. "There ain't no wimps in this family. We're Colorado royalty! Did you know that, Veda?"

Veda nodded. "I sure did." Then she turned to Arthur. "I gotta be home by four fifteen."

"Then let's go," said Arthur.

CHAPTER SEVEN

Universal Trash was huge.

From the office, Arthur and Veda hung a right beyond the art gallery on the back wall, and then past Lighting, Small Appliances, and Housewares till they arrived at Dining Room Furniture. There they took their usual spots at an antique oak table in good condition but, according to Dad, "too big and too ornate for contemporary tastes."

The table's original price, $750, had been crossed out, as had $500 and $375. The current tag read: *Make an offer!*

Sometimes Arthur found himself caring about a piece of merchandise the way a little kid cares about a teddy bear, or his grandmother cared about her motorcycle. And when the price fell and fell on something he liked, Arthur felt sad, like a friend was being insulted.

Arthur knew that was crazy. This table, just for an

example, didn't care about *him*. This table didn't care about itself. Heaped with silver and polished, or chopped up into firewood, it was all the same to the table.

Arthur knew this in his head, but in his heart he didn't believe it.

As usual on Sunday afternoons, Dad or Randolph or Jennifer Y—they were the two clerks—had set up Arthur and Veda's work station, and everything they needed was waiting for them: soft cloths for cleaning, plain white stickers, price tags, pens, index cards, a stapled printout of the UUI sort criteria, and, in a heap on a stained old cloth, the jewelry from the Carson estate.

Arthur and Veda's job was to enter each brooch, necklace, pair of earrings, barrette, and bracelet into the UUI, Universal Universal Inventory. This meant they made an index card encoding the piece according to certain sort criteria, wrote the code on a sticker, and attached the sticker to a price tag on the jewelry.

The sort criteria included appraisal (how much Dad thought the item was worth) and provenance (where it came from). Veda hadn't known any of that when she'd first come to work for Universal Trash. She hadn't known the going rate for an old pair of fake pearl earrings; a set of four wineglasses; or a linen tablecloth, still in the original packaging, either. Now, a year later, she knew all that; she was a pro.

Arthur took a blue-and-gold enamel bracelet from the pile. Veda took a pair of silver hoop earrings. They wiped the treasures with a cloth, looked them over, grabbed pens and cards, wrote quickly in small, neat letters.

This is what Arthur wrote about his bracelet:

043023AJ

S, J, C, Bt, bg

Carson

$1.25

The first line meant April 30, 2023; that he, Arthur, had made the file card; and that it was jewelry.

The next line meant it was small [S] (not an appliance [A], or an electronic [E], or a piece of visual art [V], or a musical instrument [M], or furniture [F], for example); that it was jewelry [J]; that it was costume [C] (not real gold or a real gem); that it was a bracelet [Bt]; that it was blue [b] and gold [g].

The next line was the consigner—the Carson estate. The contact information for Carson, and everyone else who left items for sale at Universal Trash, had been written on another card at the same time the lot of items had come in.

The last entry was price. Arthur hadn't had to think much about that. Unless it was special in some way, all bracelets started at one dollar and twenty-five cents. After a couple of months the price dropped to a dollar, or seventy-five cents if there were too many on hand. Two months after that, if the bracelet was still there, somebody would box it up with other unsold merchandise and haul it to a charity.

It took Arthur about a minute to write a card for the blue-and-gold bracelet, attach a tag to it, put a sticker on the tag, and place the bracelet in a bin on the floor. Either Dad or one of the clerks would take it from there, arrange the tagged jewelry in a display case to sell, and file the index cards in the UUI master system, which was contained in the index-card boxes on the shelves in the office.

Arthur reached for a pair of rhinestone earrings at the same time Veda grabbed a fake turquoise necklace. When Veda had first come to work, the two of them had competed over who could tag the most items. Then Dad had complained that their handwriting was so sloppy, he couldn't read the index cards, and they'd slowed down, and now their output was almost identical, right around one hundred items each in a two-hour shift, with a ten-minute snack break in the middle.

The work wasn't hard, but it held your attention. Arthur and Veda were barely aware of customers drifting in and out, the bell on the entrance door tinkling. They had been at it for about half an hour when two guys, maybe in their twenties, came over to check out dining room furniture.

"OMG, can you believe this place?" one said to the other.

"I know, right? I don't know what to look at first."

"Do you kids *work* here?" The first guy—who had a neat black beard and a buzz cut—paused by the old dining table and smiled at Arthur and Veda.

Arthur put on his best customer-service smile.

"We do, yes," he said. "And welcome to Universal Trash."

"We saw that ad, the one on the bus?" the second guy said. He was a little more rumpled than the first. "Something about the earth? And we thought that made sense, so here we are, and, um . . . if you don't mind, what is it you guys are *doing* exactly?"

With practiced efficiency Arthur explained. Veda, meanwhile, dropped a tagged red pendant into the bin and reached for a beaded bracelet.

"Oh, wow, that's so old-fashioned!" the first guy said.

"It is, but it works," Arthur said. "My grandpa came up with it when he and my grandmother started the store a long time ago."

"Before *computers*?" The slightly rumpled guy couldn't believe it.

"I just love this place." The bearded guy looked around as if he were in a church; then he cracked up.

"Look at *this*," he said to his friend.

On the wall by the window was a framed poster, a motto scrawled by Grandpa long ago:

Herein the collected work of humankind

Some of it useful

Much of it useless

All of it for sale

The rumpled guy grinned. "Suits me," he said. "We may be here awhile."

Having almost grown up in the store, Arthur sometimes

forgot it was awesome. Now he looked around too. The building was essentially a well-insulated warehouse with windows on the street side. What made it special was the inventory. Dad did his best to rotate goods out quickly if they didn't sell, but even so, it was packed full, and the variety of goods, the colors, the shapes and sizes—the sheer abundance of *stuff*—hit some visitors hard.

Over the table where Veda and Arthur sat, for example, hung a constellation of crystal chandeliers, seven altogether, among a couple dozen lesser lighting fixtures made of ceramic, brass, fabric, aluminum, glass, porcelain, and even calfskin.

Surrounding Arthur and Veda's big table were smaller tables in all styles, some of them set up for a holiday meal with floral centerpieces, salt and pepper shakers, crystal goblets, silver place settings, china platters, china dishes. The aisle leading away from the dining room furniture held more crystal, more silver, more china. "Decades of wedding presents, mostly unused," according to Arthur's dad.

And that was just one corner!

Beyond Dining Room Furniture was Living Room Furniture, and beyond that, most of it hanging from the wall, was the section they called Wildlife, dead wildlife more accurately. The centerpiece was an African lion, its mouth open in either a yawn or a roar. An exception to Dad's rule about rotating stock, it had presided since before Arthur was born. The price tag, which never changed, read *$5,000.* Occasionally someone asked about buying it, but so far no one had followed through.

Surrounding the lion were more heads: elk, bighorn sheep, and lots of deer, all of them with impressive antlers. On the shelves below were taxidermy mounts, whole animals posed to look like they might have in the wild: beavers, coyotes, foxes, raccoons, minks, birds, and snakes.

For a while they'd had a prairie dog mount, two little guys posed on hind legs as if they were sniffing the air. But prairie dogs were controversial in Boulder, and when a pro–prairie dog group threatened to picket the store, Dad had, somehow, made the little guys disappear.

The wildlife always attracted attention, but now the bearded guy's eyes turned to a painting in the gallery, located on the same wall as the entrance. "Is that one for real?" he asked. Arthur swiveled and saw that he meant a blotchy copy of a painting by the artist Vincent van Gogh, the one called *The Starry Night.* The real thing was in a museum somewhere, Arthur thought, worth millions of dollars. This was probably a high school art project.

"It's a real painting, and it's for sale," Arthur said. "If it's perfect for your apartment, I can offer you an excellent price."

"It might be!" The bearded guy was enthused. "Let's take a look," he said to his friend. "This place is incredible!"

Arthur logged one more piece of jewelry, a diamond necklace made of plastic, before Veda said, "Let's eat," and it was time for their snack.

nacks were located in the mini-fridge by the cash counter. There, Dad was completing the sale of a movie camera so big and heavy that it must've been ancient.

"That's a great item there," Dad told the customer, a college-aged guy, who said goodbye with a grin that announced he had made a life-changing find. "Sometimes," Dad turned to Arthur and Veda, "this job makes ya happy. Isn't that right, guys?"

"Chocolate milk makes me happy," Arthur said. "How about you, Darth?" He looked at Veda, who used to complain when he called her "Darth" but had finally decided she liked it.

"Job's good," she said, "but plain milk's better than chocolate."

By now she had set out the snack on the counter: graham crackers with peanut butter, apple slices, and milk—chocolate for Arthur, regular for Veda. It was an ordinary snack, but it looked special, the milk in teacups with saucers, the food on china plates, cloth napkins on the side. Veda was no girly girl, but she did love a tea party.

"How much did you get for the camera, Mr. Popper?" Veda asked.

"It was marked a hundred, but I gave it to him for fifty. Who knows? Maybe he'll mention the store when he wins an Oscar."

"So how does it work with the consigner if you lower the price?" Veda asked.

Arthur's dad smiled. He liked it when Veda asked business questions. "If we lower it because the item's been sitting, then we lower the payment to the consigner, too. It's in the contract. But if it's an impulse thing, like what I just did with Amy Merdle's camera, then I pay out the full amount," he said.

"Amy Merdle—the prairie dog lady?" Veda asked Arthur.

Arthur nodded. "The one who visits second-grade classes with pictures of prairie dog towns. She's a regular customer."

"I don't remember much about the slides," Veda said.

"But she had earrings in the shape of prairie dogs."

"Old friend of Arthur's grandparents' too," Dad added. "Since she moved out of her big house, she's been bringing us a lot."

Back when Arthur's grandparents founded Universal Trash, most of the merchandise had been what they picked up themselves at yard sales or from estates. Now most items came in on consignment. That is, someone brought something to the store for the store to sell. When it did, the store kept half the money and sent the rest to the consigner, the person who had brought it in.

While Arthur and Veda were eating, Randolph came over with the two guys Arthur had been talking to earlier.

"We're buying the painting!" the bearded one announced.

"Along with a few other odds and ends." His friend nodded at an almost-full shopping cart.

"Uh-*huh*," Randolph said, clearly delighted with these new customers. He was grandparent-aged and skinny, with a scraggly white beard and matching hair he cut himself. He had been working at the store for about a year, but he'd hung around before that. Now he stood beside Arthur. "I'll ring y'up if I can just shove this freeloader out of the way."

"Hey, I'm working!" Arthur protested.

"We can vouch for that," the bearded guy said.

Randolph said, "Hmmph," but he was teasing. "I could use some counter space *if* you two don't mind?"

"We gotta get back to it, anyway," Veda said.

"Almost ten after," Dad said.

"We're going," Veda said. "Come on, Arthur. I have to be home by—"

"Four fifteen. I *know*," Arthur said.

"Thanks for keeping my kid in line, Veda," Dad said.

"No problem. I'm used to it," said Veda.

CHAPTER NINE

Arthur was just marking *$2.50* on a double strand of glass pearls, the last piece from the Carson consignment, when Officer Bernstein showed up. He was standing in the Housewares aisle, staring at a red pepper mill. As if he felt Arthur's eyes on him, he turned his head. "Hello, Arthur. Hello, Veda. How's things?"

Officer Len Bernstein was a middle-aged white man with an ordinary, slightly pudgy face and thinning light brown hair. He wasn't tall or short, fat or thin, handsome or ugly. His expression was always pleasant but a little sad, as if he expected disappointment. He must not have been on duty that day, because he wasn't in uniform.

Veda and Arthur told Officer Bernstein that things were good.

"Are you interested in that pepper mill, Officer Bernstein?" Arthur asked. "It's European-made, you know, fifteen dollars retail at least, and in very good condition. I think the sticker says three dollars, but I'm sure we could arrange for the friends-and-family discount. Call it two seventy-five plus tax."

"Thank you, Arthur. It is nice," Officer Bernstein said. "But if you want to know the truth, I was wondering how many peppercorns it holds."

Officer Bernstein had a thing about numbers.

Arthur said, "Depends on how big the grains are?"

Officer Bernstein nodded—a little sadly. Meanwhile, Veda had stood up. "I have to be home by—"

"I *know*," Arthur said. "What for, anyway?"

"Watch the niños," Veda said. "Mamá has a *date*."

"Seriously?" Arthur said. He knew Mrs. Lopez was single, but he had never heard of her having a date before. "With a man?"

"Yes, a man," Veda said. "He's been working for her a while, but I haven't met him. Now I have to see if he's okay."

Arthur had other friends with single parents and divorced parents and dating parents. Still, he couldn't imagine what that would be like, meeting someone your mom *liked*, someone who wasn't your dad. "Wow," he said. "Wow. Okay. I'll see you at school, then."

Veda said goodbye to Officer Bernstein and headed for the office, where she'd left her bike.

Arthur stood up too, gathered the pens, stickers, price tags, and index cards, and headed back to the cash counter.

Officer Bernstein set down the pepper grinder—a little sadly—and went with him. Randolph was telling a customer about the store's toy-sanitizing protocol, but as soon as he saw Officer Bernstein, he narrowed his eyes and looked away. Randolph did not like Officer Bernstein because once, long ago, something had happened between them. Arthur didn't know what, and his parents wouldn't tell him.

Sometimes, Arthur thought, being a kid was a pain. Claiming they wanted to protect you, grown-ups acted all mysterious. Instead of feeling protected, you felt confused.

"Is your dad around, do you know?" Officer Bernstein asked Arthur.

Randolph interrupted his sanitized-toy talk to say, "Office."

"I know the way," Officer Bernstein said. "See you soon, Arthur. Good to see you, too, Randolph."

Randolph ignored him.

The direct route back to the entrance took Arthur

through Fine China. In general Arthur knew the store's inventory pretty well, and at that moment he knew china really well. He and Jennifer Y had rotated and restocked it the previous week.

Which was why, when he saw the teacup, he knew it was not supposed to be there.

CHAPTER TEN

The teacup rested among dozens more on a shelf just beneath Arthur's eye level. It was white and decorated with a picture of a blue cartoon bear. It might have been marching or dancing. It certainly was grinning. The cup was supposed to have a saucer, Arthur thought as he looked it over. There was a chip on the rim above the blue bear's right ear.

Other cups were on the shelf too, all in sets of six or eight, all complete with saucers.

"See something good?" Done with the customer, Randolph approached from the toy aisle.

Arthur showed him the teacup, and Randolph grinned.

"You know what that bear is, don't you, Arthur?"

Arthur thought it looked familiar. "Maybe?" he said.

"He's dancing to the beat of the HoneyJams. A long time ago, they were—"

"—a rock 'n' roll band," Arthur said. "Got it." His

grandparents had been huge fans, had met at a concert nearby in Denver. Once a year some of the old musicians still played at the stadium on campus, and his grandparents always dragged Arthur's parents, and Arthur's parents always complained that the show went on *forever.*

"But what's the cup doing here, I wonder?" Arthur said. "Dad would never take a chipped cup without a saucer."

Randolph shrugged. "Can't answer that one. See you tomorrow?"

Arthur said, "Probably," then reversed direction and headed to the office. His dad was seated at his desk with Officer Bernstein across from him. Grandpa was seated at his own desk, shifting index cards from one box to another.

Dad looked up when Arthur came in. "Done for the day?" he asked. "I think your mom is home."

"I found this in Fine China." Arthur held up the cup.

His dad saw the chip right away, shook his head. "I'll check the UUI in a bit," he said.

"I can do it right now," Grandpa said, turned to face Arthur, got a look at the teacup. When he did, his eyes widened. "No way," he said.

"No way what?" Dad asked.

"Bring that here right now, Arthur," Grandpa said.

Used to Grandpa's commands, Arthur obeyed. Grandpa took the cup, flipped it upside down, then right side up, set it on the desk, inhaled, exhaled, shook his head. All this time, it was silent in the office. What could be so important about a teacup?

"That's the one, though. I remember the chip was just in that spot," Grandpa said. "Where did you find it, Arthur?"

Arthur told him.

Dad said, "I'm missing something here."

"Should I look into it?" Officer Bernstein asked. "The case of the found teacup?"

Arthur brushed his bangs out of his eyes. This was probably a joke, he thought, but Officer Bernstein didn't smile, so it was hard to tell.

Meanwhile, Grandpa stood up, crossed to the wall of shelves that held the UUI boxes, picked out the one for Housewares, opened it, and, one by one, flipped through the cards. Arthur knew exactly where he was looking: Fine China, subcategory Tea Sets.

"No entry," Grandpa said after a moment. "Not that I really expected one." He closed the box, then turned to face the room. "Who'd have thought that after all this time the thief would bring it back?"

CHAPTER ELEVEN

What thief?" Arthur thought this sounded interesting.

Grandpa's usual state of crankiness returned. "Well, if I knew *that*, I'd know where it came from, wouldn't I?"

Arthur said, "Uh . . . I don't know, Grandpa B."

"Tell the story, Byron. If you don't mind, that is," Dad said.

Grandpa returned to his desk and sat down. "That teacup," he began, "is legendary."

No one spoke.

"That teacup," he continued, "is where Universal Trash began."

"No lie?" Impressed, Dad looked at the teacup too.

"Your grandmother found it in the trash, Arthur. The cup was chipped even then, but she thought somebody would want it, a Breadhead, you know. And we were hard up. Down to our last jar of peanut butter, no gas in the van, and gas was sixty cents a gallon in those days."

"What's a Breadhead?" Arthur asked.

Grandpa chuckled, something he did not do often. "It's what we devoted fans of the HoneyJams used to call ourselves. Jam goes with bread, get it? And they were a jam band, and . . ." He shrugged. "It seemed funny at the time."

"Go on, Byron," Dad said.

"Well, we figured we'd sell the teacup for a dollar, buy a couple of apples, a little gas, drive on to the next show. We had no idea of making a real business, you understand."

Officer Bernstein looked thoughtful. Sad but also thoughtful. "With gas at sixty cents," he said, "a dollar buys you one and two-thirds gallons. Say the van got twenty-five miles to the gallon—that's forty miles."

Grandpa nodded. "Which is why I had the bright idea of making up some nonsense about how Jerry Strange himself used to play tea party with that cup when he was just a little guy."

"Jerry Strange was the lead singer of the HoneyJams," Dad said to Arthur.

"I *know* that, Dad."

"Just making sure," Dad said.

"But that story doesn't make any sense, Grandpa," Arthur said. "The bear was a cartoon for the HoneyJams. And they didn't exist yet when Jerry Strange was a little kid."

"It was a tall tale," Grandpa said. "What do you want from me? The point was, it made the cup special, so we could charge more. Five dollars, I think we asked."

"Eight and a third gallons," Officer Bernstein said.

"We scrounged a few more items too," Grandpa said. "T-shirts and earrings, if I remember, beads probably, and we cleaned it all up, put it all out on the only table we owned—a card table with a wobbly leg—added price tags, told everybody it was high-quality stuff, the teacup especially . . . and what do you know, it worked. We made . . . ten dollars? I think it was ten dollars. We felt like we were rolling in dough."

"But someone stole the teacup?" Arthur asked.

Grandpa gave him a look.

"Sorry," Arthur said.

Grandpa resumed. "Someone musta believed my tall tale because the teacup disappeared. Your grandmother and I musta been busy with something else, and somebody

46

snatched it. We laughed at the time. We could afford to. We had our fortune, our ten dollars. We didn't mind so much that we had been ripped off."

Arthur nodded, but he was still confused. "Then what happened?"

"What do you mean, 'Then what happened?'" Grandpa B was cranky again, his usual self. "We grew up, we opened the store on Valmont, we had a kid. . . . Somewhere in there we got married. Then we got old."

"I mean what happened to the teacup?" Arthur persisted.

"Have you been paying attention?" Grandpa said. "I don't know what happened to the teacup, not till today when it shows up out of nowhere."

"So you think the thief brought it back?" Arthur asked.

"How do I know what thieves do?" Grandpa asked.

"Crazy story, Byron," Dad said.

"So that's . . . what?" Officer Bernstein seemed to be calculating. "You founded the store in the '80s, so more than forty years the teacup has been missing."

"Can I have it?" Arthur asked.

Grandpa shrugged. "Makes no difference to me now."

"You need a chipped teacup?" Dad asked.

Arthur was thinking the cup was the right size for a certain mouse he knew, a ghost mouse. It would be a place for her to hang out. Since he couldn't say that, he said, "The bear is funny."

Dad shrugged. "Sure, Arthur. Go ahead and take it. That teacup might be legendary, but in terms of resale? A chipped teacup is worthless."

CHAPTER TWELVE

Upstairs the whole apartment smelled like the chili Arthur's mom had put on the stove before she'd left for the office. On Sundays she always said she was going to work "just for a couple of hours" and then spent most of the day at the office. After Dad hung out the closed signs and locked the store, he'd come up and make something for dessert.

Arthur's mom was not in the kitchen, so Arthur walked through it and down the hall to his own bedroom, teacup in hand.

"Whatcha got there?" Close to Arthur's right ear, Watson's voice startled him. When he looked, she was perched on his shoulder.

"Teacup," Arthur said, and placed it on a shelf between his collection of Sherlock Holmes books and a clay pig he'd made in preschool. "It's your size, I think. I could put some cotton in it or something. A piece of handkerchief? Like a hangout for you, I guess."

"How thoughtful, Arthur. Thank you," Watson said. "I'll check it out, if I might."

Arthur noticed that Watson seemed to have two speeds, quick and stop. When he placed her in the teacup, she nosed around in a hurry, then came to rest, perfectly still, her bright eyes peeking over the rim. "Just the right size," she said.

Arthur was pleased he had thought of it.

"So what's new?" he asked, taking a seat on the edge of his bed.

"Not a lot," Watson admitted. "Now that I don't have a body to feed and exercise, I have time on my hands. Perhaps I'll spend it contemplating life's mysteries."

Arthur nodded. "I have some mysteries you could contemplate if you want."

"Yes?" Watson said.

"I mean, since you're a ghost, can you tell the future? Or maybe read minds? It would be cool if you could. I mean, if you're supposed to be helping me? That would be helpful. Like in school or life or whatever."

Watson tugged her whiskers. "I don't think I can tell the future," she said after a moment. "But go ahead and ask your questions."

Most of Arthur's questions weren't school stuff at all but questions about people. What made Officer Bernstein sad? Why was Grandpa B cranky and embarrassing? How come his mom was always at work?

But those questions were hard. Maybe he should start with an easier one.

So, since he was looking right at the teacup, he explained (short version) how it had disappeared and come back. "Do you know who the thief is?" he asked.

"No idea," Watson said. "Perhaps it's like a puzzle to solve, a mystery."

"I like mysteries," Arthur said. "For a fact, mystery books are what I usually check out of the library. I've even read one grown-up one by a writer named Christie something. The plot was kind of tough to follow, but the ending was good."

"I believe that would be Agatha Christie," Watson said. "She's very famous and, like me, she's dead."

"Oh, that's too bad," Arthur said. "I mean, I guess it is. Anyway, the mystery of the teacup isn't a very big one—not like something in a book or a movie, with murder or missing diamonds and whatnot."

"No, not like that," Watson admitted. "Still, it's rather

fun to solve a puzzle. Mice, of course, are famous for their navigating mazes, which are a kind of puzzle. Perhaps if you solve the mystery of the teacup, you will feel a glowing sense of accomplishment."

"I'm not sure I've ever felt that before," Arthur said.

Still, he was a little disappointed that Watson hadn't simply answered the question.

CHAPTER THIRTEEN

A t school the next day Veda updated Arthur on Juan, the guy her mom had had a date with.

"He has *a lot* of tattoos," Veda said. "Do you know how much tattoos cost? How come he spends money on that, anyway? Mamá has only four tattoos, one for me and one for each of the niños, and all the tattoos are tiny."

Arthur shook his head. "I never saw 'em, I don't think."

"Because they're *tiny*," Veda said, "which is appropriate for a mom."

"But besides the tattoos, he was okay?" Arthur asked. He and Veda were in different sixth-grade homerooms, but they had library time together. Now they were in line to check out books. Veda was carrying the maximum number, six. Arthur had one.

"I guess," Veda said. "I didn't like the way he smiled at my mom, though. He looked too cheerful—like a puppy."

"Eww," said Arthur.

At the checkout desk Mrs. Danneberg, the librarian, looked at Arthur's book. "Another mystery," she said.

"Is that bad?" Arthur asked.

"No, no. It's not bad at all," she said. "Only, I keep thinking one day you'll want to read about your namesake, King Arthur."

"My grandma told me about him," Arthur said. "He lived a long time ago, and his friends were named 'Merlin' and 'Lancelot.' Oh, and he was a king."

Mrs. Danneberg rolled her eyes. She did that a lot. "Right, Arthur. But there is more to learn about him than that. Did you know, for example, that as a kid he was called 'the Wart'?"

"That sounds very interesting, Mrs. Danneberg," Arthur said, at the same time that he was thinking warts were pretty gross. "Maybe next week I'll get a King Arthur book."

Mrs. Danneberg sighed and pulled Arthur's choice across the checkout desk. "Next week."

At lunch Arthur always sat at the same outdoor table in the picnic pavilion with the same guys, Ethan, Danh, and

Zeke. Last year he could've sat with Veda, but this year sitting with a girl was not okay. Veda seemed to understand this too. They had never talked about it. They just started sitting with other people.

Ethan, Danh, and Zeke were like Arthur, a little uncool. They were okay at sports but not great, okay-looking but not great, and they didn't travel to Vail or Jackson or any of the other fancy ski destinations on weekends in the winter. If their moms drove on a field trip, it wasn't in a new Tesla but in a plain Toyota, and their fleeces were plain Columbia or hand-me-down Patagonia, not Stio or Montbell or any of the cooler labels.

Arthur got along with most of the guys in his class, even if none of them knew anything about customer service, even if Arthur didn't know a lot about mountain bikes or video games besides the obvious ones. By sixth grade they had been together long enough, had written enough skits together and built enough science fair projects and spoken enough Spanish dialogues, that they were used to each other.

That day at lunch Zeke announced that he'd played *Super Smash Bros.* for six straight hours the day before.

"So that's why your butt's getting big," Arthur said

without thinking. "'Cause it's always stuck to your chair."

"Bi-i-i-ig Butt *Super Smash*!" Ethan said. "That's what we'll call you from now on, Zeke."

"All right, guys, sheez, come on," Zeke mumbled. "It's not like—"

"Whatta ya got in your lunch, Big Butt?" Danh asked.

Arthur wasn't even listening by this time. Dad had packed chocolate chip cookies that day, and Arthur was thinking about cookies. Danh and Ethan kept on with the joke for a couple more minutes, but it wasn't that funny, and soon they forgot all about it.

What Arthur didn't know was that Zeke actually worried that his butt might be getting big. And Zeke did not forget.

CHAPTER FOURTEEN

That afternoon the school bus dropped Arthur off a block from the store at the usual time, three forty. At four he would check in with his dad to see if the store needed him to help out. Between, he took a walk on a nearby trail around a lake so small that it ought to have been called a pond, only everyone was used to calling it a lake.

While he walked, he made a plan to tell Veda about Watson. He didn't know how she'd react, if she'd think he'd lost it, if she'd refer him to the school counselor, or want to talk to his mom or something.

Still, he usually did tell Veda stuff, and it would be weird not to tell her about how a mouse had decided to haunt him. Being haunted by a mouse was unusual.

Arthur also looked out for prairie dogs and other critters—birds, rabbits, squirrels. And he worried about mountain lions. Everyone knew you shouldn't run if you saw one. You should make yourself as big as possible, raise your arms over your head, stomp and shout, and act like you were the boss.

Arthur did not like to fight. Not with the guys at lunch or his mom or even Ramona. Faced with a mountain lion, he would probably run.

Back at the store Arthur opened the entrance door, heard the sound of chimes, and saw there were lots of customers.

"Oh, Arthur! Good!" Dad said when he saw him. "Randolph's not feeling well, so I sent him home. Then, naturally, Jennifer and I got slammed. How about helping this nice lady with some crystal? She's a brand-new customer."

"Sure thing," Arthur said, and smiled brightly. The lady was mom-aged or a little older, fit-looking and wearing the Boulder uniform of jeans, hiking boots, and a T-shirt.

"I need a wedding present," she said. "Very traditional wedding, and I heard that ad you've got going. I mean, I want to save the earth. Who doesn't?"

"Happy to help, ma'am," Arthur said. "We have an amazing selection."

The brand-new customer examined a dozen possibilities before choosing a cut-crystal bowl.

"You've made a fine choice," Arthur said. "It's not only pretty, it's useful. And a fraction of the price of buying new."

Back at the cash counter he learned the brand-new customer's name—Susana Malarky—from her credit card.

"The bride will never know it's used, right?" Susana said. "Or, more important, her mother won't know?"

"Get a nice box and plenty of tissue," Arthur advised. "The only people likely to recognize something from our stock are our regular customers."

"I don't think the mother of the bride would *ever* shop here," Susana said. "No offense or anything, but some people, people like *her*, they think it's . . . tacky? To buy stuff used?"

"We prefer the word 'vintage,'" Arthur said.

Susana nodded. "That's a good way to say it," she said. "There's a woman in my book club, older lady, I think maybe she used to own this store?"

"I bet you mean my grandmother," Arthur said. "And my mom's Jeri. She's in the same book group too."

Susana Malarky had a canvas bag slung over her shoulder. She reached in, dug around, pulled out a library book. Arthur read the title: *Of Mice and Men* by John Steinbeck.

"I haven't started it yet," she said. "Do you know if your mom has? Or your grandmother? It's pretty short, so I think I can finish it in time."

Arthur finished with the receipt and wrapped the bowl in paper to protect it. "My grandmother's away, so I don't know about her," he said. "My mom's always busy."

Susana Malarky looked around one last time, a little awestruck the way first-time customers often were. "Ha— that's funny," she said, and took a step toward the jewelry case at the right of the register.

"May I get something out for you?" Arthur asked.

"Oh, no. Not necessary." She shook her head. "It's just that those earrings"—she nodded at some gold pendants—"remind me of some I got from my mother. I never wear them. They just sit around in my jewelry box."

Arthur imagined earrings sitting around, and smiled. Then he put the wrapped bowl into a bag and handed it across the counter. "Receipt's inside. I hope the happy couple enjoy their present. And thank you for shopping at Universal Trash."

When Susana Malarky had said goodbye, Arthur placed the crystal bowl's price tag in a box with the others from that day. Later someone—Dad, Grandpa, or Laura the bookkeeper—would credit fifteen dollars to the consigner and move the card to another box in the UUI system, the one for items recently sold.

Universal Trash was open till six p.m. on weekdays. By six fifteen Jennifer had left and Dad had hung the closed sign in the window. "Pizza? Or tacos?" he asked Arthur.

"Pizza," Arthur said. "Can we get it from Locale? I know it's more expensive, but—"

"We deserve Locale," Dad said. "Maybe your mom can pick it up. And a salad, too, for good health."

"Is Grandpa B coming?" Arthur asked. "I mean, I'm just wondering. I love Grandpa and everything, but—"

This conversation took place while Arthur and his dad climbed the stairs. "Not tonight," Dad said, tugging off his shoes in the mudroom. "And I love him too—in theory."

Upstairs in his room, Arthur considered his homework.

"I can do it in half an hour," he said out loud. "Less, probably."

"Do what?" Watson asked.

Caught talking to himself, Arthur must have blushed, because Watson continued, "Don't be embarrassed, Arthur! It's a waste of energy! I, for one, talk to myself all the time. I find I am a good conversationalist too."

Arthur looked around, saw that Watson was lying on her back in her teacup, her tail draped over the rim.

"You are," Arthur agreed.

"Now tell me," Watson went on, "what did you learn today? A creature should learn something every day, you know."

Arthur thought for a moment. In social studies there'd been a quiz about the countries of South America, but he still wasn't sure which was the long skinny one, Bolivia or Chile, so he didn't want to say that. Also, would Watson care about the countries of South America?

"Well," Arthur said, "recently I learned that when prairie dogs chirp, they communicate complicated stuff to each other, like 'Coyote coming!' or 'That human with a hat won't hurt you.'"

Watson rubbed her whiskers. "Interesting," she said. "Not surprising, though. In general people don't give rodents enough credit."

Arthur thought that was probably true.

"So have you thought any more about that mystery of ours?" Watson asked. "Where did my teacup come from?"

"I haven't really," Arthur said. "It's only been a day, and I had school, and then I helped out in the store." He shrugged. In fact he was pretty busy, but at the same time he felt bad. If he wanted that glowing sense of accomplishment, he would have to work harder. "What about you?" he asked Watson. "Have you thought about it?"

Watson admitted she had not. "You're the mystery fan," she said, "which means you're the one who needs to investigate!"

Arthur wasn't sure he liked being ordered around by a mouse. Still, he had asked for help. "Sure, Watson," he said.

"Watson?" Ramona was standing in the doorway. "Who's Watson? And why are you talking to a teacup?"

Arthur felt embarrassed and took it out on his sister. "Never mind," he snapped.

"*Fine!*" Ramona snapped back. "So I won't tell you that Mom is home with the pizza."

CHAPTER FIFTEEN

Dinner was almost over when Ramona announced, "Arthur talks to teacups."

"No, I don't," Arthur said truthfully.

"Then who's Watson?" Ramona asked.

Arthur's dad took a sip of beer. "Your brother can talk to teacups if he wants to, Ramona. And he can have an imaginary friend, too."

"But I *don't*—" Arthur began.

"So I can have an imaginary friend?" Ramona interrupted.

"Yes," Dad said.

"Do *you* have an imaginary friend, Daddy?" Ramona asked.

"I have your mother." Dad dabbed his lips with his napkin.

Ramona looked at her mother.

Her mother shook her head. "I am not imaginary, Ramona. In case you were going to ask."

Arthur cracked up. "Good one, Mom."

Ramona didn't seem to be listening. "My imaginary friend is named Bluebell," she said.

"There's one more piece of pizza," Mom said.

Arthur and his dad both reached for it.

"Split it or fight?" Dad asked Arthur.

"Fight," Arthur said, and they pumped their fists and spoke in unison. "Rock! Paper! Scissors! Shoot!"

Dad's scissors beat Arthur's paper. "Better luck next time, kid." Dad took the pizza, opened his mouth to take a bite, caught Mom's look.

"One of you is still growing," Mom said.

Dad set the pizza on his plate, cut it in two, gave half to Arthur. Arthur ate it in three bites.

"Bluebell is a cow," Ramona said. "And she's blue. In case that isn't obvious."

"Does her milk taste like blueberries?" Dad asked.

Ramona's eyebrows made a *V. "Eww,"* she said. "No."

Dad shrugged one shoulder. "Just asking." By now his half slice of pizza was gone too. "My turn to do dishes. Arthur, what's the homework sitch?"

"Hardly anything," Arthur said.

"Which means math," Mom said. "Get to it, then. And,

Ramona, maybe you'd like to draw a picture of Bluebell before bed?"

Ramona sighed. "I'd rather draw Watson," she said. "Only, I don't know what Watson is."

Ramona had a lot more after-school activities than Arthur did—soccer, swimming, chess club, and story camp. Arthur was glad about this because on the rare occasions when she was home and he was not, Ramona had been known to invade Arthur's space. Now he was afraid she might decide to investigate the mysterious Watson when he wasn't home, so for the next few days he was extra vigilant about his room.

As far as he could tell, though, no Ramona invasion took place. There was never a telltale girly smell, never a drawer left half-open or a colored pencil missing from the mug on the windowsill.

Maybe Ramona was busier than usual? Or maybe she had lost interest in his "imaginary friend."

Friday was Cinco de Mayo, and Carpenter Elementary celebrated with free churros at lunch. Walking to social studies, Veda told Arthur that Juan was coming over to celebrate with her family, which meant her mom would be seeing him two days in a row, and didn't that seem like a lot?

"Do the niños like him okay?" Arthur asked.

"They laugh at his jokes," Veda said.

"Do you laugh?" Arthur asked.

Veda shrugged. "He's kind of funny."

Arthur thought in that case maybe Juan was not so bad, even if he did spend too much money on tattoos. But Arthur didn't say so. "Can you come over early on Sunday?" he asked. "I know you have swimming, but there's, uh . . . stuff I want to talk about."

"Are you okay?" Veda could turn mom-like in an instant.

"Nothing bad," Arthur said. "Just something I'm thinking about, is all."

"My hair'll be wet," Veda said.

"And you'll smell like chlorine." Arthur wrinkled his nose. "But that's okay."

CHAPTER SIXTEEN

D ad asked Arthur to help out in the store again that day. It wasn't super busy, but both Grandpa and Jennifer were taking the afternoon off. Grandpa wasn't feeling well, and Jen was a trail runner, a serious one, with a hundred-mile race in the mountains coming up. Today she had to run some ridiculous distance like thirty-five miles.

Even if you were fast and tough like Jen, it took hours to run so far.

"With so much business, we've gotten behind on cleaning," Dad told Arthur. "Randolph is over in Toys, if you want to join him."

Arthur said, "Sure." He liked working in the store. It wasn't only that he was good at customer service. He also liked that he'd been doing it a long time, which made the tasks familiar and comfortable.

Arthur liked the familiar and the comfortable.

If you had asked him what he admired about Veda, he would have told you he admired her for being a loyal friend and interesting to talk to. He would *not* have told you that he admired her for being brave and trying new things, but actually he did.

In short, Veda was adventurous, and Arthur worried that he was not. If that was true, would there be only the familiar and the comfortable forever? Maybe he'd be working in the store forever.

He knew that was what his family expected. His dad had told him so often enough, and his grandpa, too.

Arthur found Randolph dusting, one by one, the tiny airplanes from a Fisher-Price airport, priced at fifteen dollars.

"Hey," Arthur said. "What can I do?"

"Take some o' that vinegar spray." Randolph nodded at the dolls on a lower shelf. "I think they could use a wipe-down."

Arthur picked up a rag and squirt bottle, grabbed a baby doll with a smudged face, and went to work.

"It's cool what Jennifer Y's doing, huh?" he said. "I can't imagine running that far."

"I wouldn't run that far," Randolph said, "not unless I was being chased."

"In the war were you chased?" Arthur knew Randolph had been a soldier. "Like, by the enemy?"

"I did some running sometimes, me and the guys in my platoon, uh-*huh.* It's not clear if we were really being chased, or just thought we were. The sitch on the ground got confusing."

"That sounds bad," Arthur said.

Randolph said, "It was," but he didn't say more, and the quiet got uncomfortable.

"What did you do after you were a soldier?" Arthur finally asked.

"Janitorial. Window washing," Randolph said. "I never had what you'd call a career. Like your family, I enjoyed the flea market thing, going to yard sales and looking for treasure, reselling it."

"Did you ever find it?" Arthur asked. "Treasure?"

"Uh-*huh,*" Randolph said. "That's a funny story."

"Tell me," Arthur said, "if you want, I mean."

Randolph climbed onto a step stool to dust the high shelves across the aisle. "It was a ring, woman's ring, with a pale blue stone," he said. "Not turquoise. An aquamarine."

"So it was real?" Arthur asked.

Randolph grinned. "Now you're getting ahead of my story."

"Sorry," Arthur said.

"The ring had a gold band and a couple o' white stones, diamonds maybe? Saw it at a yard sale over on Pine. They had a ton of stuff, ninety-nine percent junk. You know."

Arthur did know.

"So I bought the ring. Marked two dollars, and I paid one. Then, lacking a lady friend, I brought it here. Except Universal Trash was closed that day. Can you guess why?"

Arthur shook his head. "We hardly ever close. I mean, it wasn't Christmas, was it?"

"Nah. It was a Saturday in October, right around seven years ago."

Arthur thought a second but still couldn't figure it out.

"A certain new family member? Your dad gave everyone the day off to celebrate."

"Oh." Arthur caught on. "Ramona."

"Uh-*huh*," Randolph said. "Your one and only sibling, Arthur. But to continue—since I didn't have what you'd call cash to spare, I chose not to wait for your dad to open up. Instead I moseyed on over to Jumper Jewelers on Pearl Street. They're picky about what they'll take, but I had a good feeling about that ring."

Arthur had moved from baby dolls to Barbies, straightening their hair, wiping their limbs, sitting them up against their Barbie cars and backpacks. "Was it worth a lot?" Arthur asked.

"You're really determined to spoil my story, aren't you?" Randolph said.

"Sorry," Arthur said again. "So what happened?"

Randolph bobbed his head. "Well you might ask! Because as quick as a wink, I was in the slammer!"

It took Arthur a moment to understand "slammer." "You had to go to *jail*?"

"Escorted by none other than your friend Officer Len Bernstein," Randolph said. "Now, what do you think of that?"

What Arthur thought was that he must have missed something. "But I don't get it. Why?"

Done with the shelves, Randolph stepped off the ladder, went to get a broom, returned, swept up a dust bunny, explained. The ring, it turned out, matched the description of one that was stolen. The jeweler recognized it and called the Boulder Police Department—the BPD.

"Officer Bernstein didn't ask too many questions," Randolph recalled. "Shady-looking character such as myself? I was presumed guilty."

"But—" Arthur was confused.

"Maybe I should mention that at the time I was what they call 'unhoused,'" Randolph continued. "I may have been a bit raggedy, an annoyance to the customers. It's possible the folks at Jumper Jewelers were not so keen on having me there."

Arthur didn't know what to say to that. There were a lot of unhoused people around, especially along the Boulder Creek Path. Seeing them made Arthur feel bad but also a little scared. They weren't like other people, right? What if one of them acted crazy, did something dangerous?

Now here it turned out his friend Randolph had been homeless—unhoused—himself.

"But you have a place to live now, right?" Arthur asked. He'd gotten away from the story of the ring, but this seemed more important.

"I do, yeah," Randolph said. "Your family helped me out, in fact. I bet you never knew that, did you?"

Arthur shook his head.

"The best people don't need to crow about it. As for the ring—"

"Oh, right." Arthur had almost forgotten. "So what happened?"

"The stones were real," Randolph said, "and so was the gold, worth around six hundred dollars all told. So, if my math is right, that'd make a sixty thousand percent return on my one-dollar investment."

Arthur thought Randolph sounded like Officer Bernstein, but he didn't say so. "That's amazing. But wait—I thought the ring was stolen?"

Randolph shook his head. "Nah, it wasn't. The stolen ring the cops had a report on was turquoise, a man's ring, in fact. Not the same at all. But an unhoused guy with a nice piece of jewelry? People jump to conclusions."

"How did you get out of jail?" Arthur asked.

"Your family again. They felt bad the whole thing happened on account o' the store being closed. With their help, it didn't take too long to straighten things out with the police."

"It was Ramona's fault, if you think about it," Arthur said.

Randolph cocked his head. "New baby? Itty-bitty thing? I don't think she picked her time to be born."

Arthur shrugged. "So in that case, the ring really was yours. Did Jumper Jewelers buy it? So then you had some money?" Arthur was used to mystery stories where the ending was happy, the detective triumphed. He hoped in real life Randolph had triumphed too.

But Randolph surprised him, shook his head. "Nah. I've been taken advantage of enough times; I didn't want to do the same to someone else. I walked the ring back to the guy over on Pine Street, told him the story. Naturally he didn't know the ring was valuable, or he wouldn't've sold it to me for a dollar. It had been sitting around in his grandma's jewelry box with a lot of other pieces. He figured it was all costume, not worth a thing."

More jewelry sitting around, Arthur thought. But wait— "Did you just give it back?" he asked.

"Of course not!" Randolph said. "That wouldn't have been fair, now, would it? I told him I wanted my dollar, and he gave it to me. The look on his face"—Randolph smiled like he was remembering—"it was pretty much worth it."

CHAPTER SEVENTEEN

Later Arthur repeated the story for Watson. This was a few minutes before dinnertime, and she was relaxing in her teacup.

"So now I know why Randolph doesn't like Officer Bernstein," Arthur said. "But both of them are good guys, so they ought to get along. I mean, that's how the world works, right? The good guys stick together."

"I'm not sure how the world works, Arthur," Watson said.

Arthur was also relaxing, lying back on his bed with his feet in the air so the blood would go to his head. Just as he liked to test words sometimes, Arthur liked to test ideas. Veda had seen somewhere that putting your feet in the air would make you smart, so he was testing this out. "Yeah, okay. Me neither," Arthur said. "I mean, till recently I never knew there were ghosts even. Or that one would haunt me. Or that she would be a mouse."

"What about my teacup, Arthur?" Watson said. "Have you been working on it?"

"Not exactly, Watson. But I will. I swear," Arthur said. And he thought that was another thing he'd never known, that the mouse that was haunting him would be so bossy.

At dinner Arthur intended to ask his parents about Randolph and the ring, but before he could, they were talking about Grandpa.

"He should see a doctor," Dad told Mom.

Arthur remembered that Grandpa hadn't been at the store that afternoon. "Is he really sick?"

"I think it's mostly stress," Mom said.

"What does he have to be stressed about?" Dad asked. "I'm the one running the store. *I* should be stressed."

"Is Grandpa gonna die?" Ramona asked.

Mom looked at her, surprised.

Ramona clarified. "It's not my question. It's Bluebell's question."

"Bluebell . . . ," Mom said. "Who's Bluebell again?"

Ramona couldn't believe it. *"Mo-o-om!"*

"Her imaginary friend," Dad said. "Remember, Jer?"

"Oh sure. Of course."

"If you remember," said Ramona, dark eyebrows knitted, "what kind of animal *is* Bluebell, anyway?"

"Uh-oh," Dad murmured.

"Trick question?" Mom tried. "She's not an animal; she's a . . . flower fairy?"

"Give it up, Mom," Arthur said.

Ramona continued to frown.

"I'm sorry, Ramona," Mom said. "What kind of animal is Bluebell? This time I won't forget."

They were having fish tacos for dinner in honor of Cinco de Mayo. Carefully Ramona forked a bite, chewed it, swallowed. Then she dabbed her lips with her napkin and said, "Never mind."

"You know what, honey?" Mom said. "Someday you are going to be a grown-up with a job too."

"I hope not," Ramona said. "I like being a kid. I don't want to have a job and be grumpy all the time."

Mom blinked, looked at Dad. "Am I grumpy all the time?"

Arthur was glad she hadn't asked him, because she kind of was, but he didn't think she wanted to hear it.

As for Arthur's dad, he avoided the question. "I don't think I wanted to grow up either," he said. "What about you, Arthur? Do you want to grow up?"

"We were talking about whether I'm grumpy!" Mom said, and she sounded pretty grumpy about it too.

"Actually, we were talking about Grandpa," Dad said, "and yes, Ramona, you can tell Bluebell that Grandpa is going to die, because we all are. But I hope not soon."

"Bluebell is a cow, Mom," Arthur said.

"Right," Mom said. "Ramona brought in pictures this morning. See? I remember all about it."

By this time the plates were empty. Dad took a last drink of beer and pushed back his chair. "When you were little, Jer, did you want to grow up?" he asked Mom.

"I couldn't wait," Mom said.

"I wasn't so interested in the idea," Dad said, "unless it meant I got to eat as much ice cream as I wanted."

"Barbecue potato chips," Arthur said. "That's what I'll eat when I'm grown-up."

"They're bad for you." Mom stood, began to clear the plates.

Arthur looked at his dad. "When you were a kid, did you think you'd work in a store like Universal Trash?"

"Not really," Dad said. "I thought I'd be a professional skateboarder. And if that didn't work out, a musician—play guitar in a band, write sad songs about love."

"You still have your guitars," said Mom, who was

loading the dishwasher. "You have practically a whole room full of guitars."

Dad nodded. "But managing the store's a bit more practical. Maybe I'm not, I don't know, adventurous enough to be a musician? And, like Arthur here, I'm good at customer service. Anyway, so I'm told."

I'd rather be adventurous, Arthur thought.

"Grandma's adventurous," Ramona said. "She's on a motorcycle adventure right now, right? Where is she, anyway?"

"Utah somewhere, last I heard," said Dad, "and I, for one, wish she'd get a move on and come back. Then maybe your grandpa would feel better."

CHAPTER EIGHTEEN

rthur asked his dad about Randolph's ring story the next afternoon. They were at the store getting ready to close, and Dad confirmed that the story was true.

"So that makes Randolph like a hero, doesn't it?" Arthur said.

"I wish Len—Officer Bernstein—saw it that way," Dad said. Then he added some other details. One was that the time Officer Bernstein arrested Randolph wasn't the first time he'd been in jail.

"What do you mean?" Arthur asked.

Dad shrugged. "He got arrested for little things. Drunk in public. Fighting maybe? I was pretty sure he was a good guy at heart, though, and that whole business with the ring showed I was right. Check the locks, would you?"

Part of closing was the walk-through, going around to make sure all the customers were gone, checking every window and the two sets of doors to see that the locks were engaged. While Arthur did that, his dad moved the cash from the register to the safe and switched the alarm system from day mode to night.

It took a few minutes. When Arthur was done, he met his dad in the office. He still had questions. "Weren't you ever, uh . . . nervous, I guess . . . about hiring a guy who'd been arrested before?" he asked.

"Randolph, you mean?" His dad shrugged. "Kiddo, remember, he didn't have a place to live, a place to sleep. How would any of us make out? Who knows what we'd do to get along, or what we'd do to defend ourselves?"

Dad's questions made Arthur think of his ancestor on the Colorado royalty side, the one who had slept out and been hungry, been poor before he was rich. Maybe Arthur's ancestor had done bad stuff too. Maybe someone had helped him the way his family had helped Randolph. But those details hadn't been passed down in the family history. They didn't fit the idea of royalty.

"Grandpa B's coming to dinner," Arthur's dad said. "Remember?"

"What? Oh." Arthur took a breath and counted to three for practice. "Okay."

"Try to be nice," Arthur's dad said. "With Grandma gone, he's having a rough time lately."

"Stress," Arthur said, remembering the conversation the night before. "You be nice too, Dad, okay?"

Dinner was macaroni and cheese, but not the kind from a box. Instead Mom had made sauce on the stove and added cheese and mixed it with cooked macaroni and put the whole thing in the oven in a casserole dish.

Arthur was in the kitchen because he was hungry. Grandpa B was seated at the table. Smiling, Mom removed the dish from the oven. The macaroni had turned out well, golden on top. It filled the kitchen with a warm and cheesy smell.

Grandpa cocked his head, looked skeptical. "Kraft was good enough for you when you were little," he said.

"Homemade is better," Mom said, "if you have the time."

"I thought you were always so busy with work," Grandpa said.

Mom ignored this. "It needs to sit for a minute to set."

"I'm hungry now," Grandpa B said.

"Tough beans," Mom said, but not very loud.

Arthur had been setting the table, counting out forks, spoons, and knives. Now he paused, wondering if he'd heard his mom right, and looked at her.

Grandpa B seemed startled. "What was that, Jeri?"

Mom didn't answer the question. "Would you like a beer?" she asked instead. "Dan usually has one at dinner."

"I thought he'd packed on a few pounds," Grandpa said.

"So no beer, then," Mom said.

"I never said that," Grandpa said.

From where he sat, Grandpa couldn't see the exasperation on Mom's face, but Arthur could, and he was glad he hadn't caused it. "Should I tell Dad and Ramona dinner's ready?" he asked her.

Mom said "What?" like she'd forgotten he was there, then, "Oh. Sure, honey. Thank you."

Grandpa's crankiness persisted after they sat down. Arthur and his parents were unusually quiet, anxious that anything they said would annoy him, but Ramona didn't know any better and asked, "Why isn't anybody talking?"

"We're talking," Dad said. "I told your mother the macaroni is delicious, didn't I?"

"You did, and thank you," Mom said.

"It is good, Mom," Arthur said.

"I like the box kind better," Ramona said. "When is Grandma coming back?"

Arthur wasn't sure, but it almost seemed like the kitchen got even quieter then, like everyone had stopped breathing. *Now we're in for it,* Arthur thought.

"If you're asking me," Grandpa B said finally, his voice like a growl, "I am sure I do not know."

"She always does come back," Dad said. "I wouldn't worry, Ramona."

"I'm not worried. I just miss her," Ramona said. "Do you miss her, Grandpa?"

Grandpa knitted his eyebrows, and for the first time Arthur noticed that they were like Ramona's, only gnarlier and white. "Pffft," he said, almost a spit. "I like being by myself. She's always reminding me to take my pills or wash up before I eat. You'd think I was a child."

Ramona stopped chewing but didn't bother to swallow. "What's wrong with being a child?" she asked thickly.

"Nothing at all," Mom said. "There's ice cream for dessert."

"Do you like ice cream, Grandpa?" Ramona asked.

Grandpa scowled. "Take it or leave it," he said.

"Speaking of being a child . . . ," Mom said.

Grandpa pounced. "What was that?"

Dad jumped up. "Sounds like my cue." And he began clearing the table.

Arthur had never been super close to his grandpa. When he'd been little, Grandpa B had still been busy with the store. Then when Ramona had come along, Arthur had noticed that most of the grown-ups made a big fuss over the little baby, but Grandpa had kept out of the way.

Arthur had asked his mom about that.

"Grandpa's just not that comfortable with babies," Mom said. "I think he's afraid he'll break them."

But Arthur was close to his grandma. On his bookshelf were the same Sherlock Holmes mystery books Grandma had read when she was growing up. When Arthur was younger, he had sat in her lap and played with her long gray hair, tugged the buttons on the colorful dresses she liked to wear, and listened to her read Sherlock Holmes. Now, sometimes, Grandma read the books to Ramona—only, according to Grandma, Ramona was not as patient as Arthur had been.

Arthur was secretly proud to be the patient one. Or did that go along with not being adventurous?

The first time Veda had met Grandma, she had told Arthur that Grandma looked like a witch, a bruja. Veda probably hadn't meant it as an insult. She'd been only six—same age as Ramona now, and six-year-old people sometimes speak without thinking.

Still, Arthur had slugged Veda. Then Veda had slugged Arthur back, and Arthur had fallen onto his butt, hadn't cried, had gotten right up, and said, "My grandmother does *not* look like a witch. That hurt. Don't hit me any more."

"So don't hit me either," Veda had said.

"I won't," Arthur had said, and they'd never hit each other again.

CHAPTER NINETEEN

A s predicted, Veda smelled like chlorine when she got to the store the next afternoon, Sunday, and her hair was wet too.

"Do you want to go for a walk?" Arthur met her by the entrance. "I mean, if you're not tired out from swimming."

"Why would I be tired out?" Veda asked. "Let's go."

Arthur hadn't been outside yet that day, and he blinked in the light. "First I want to show you something," he said as they crossed the parking lot. "Then we can walk on the trail around the lake."

They stopped by Mouse 4's grave. Arthur thought that would be a good lead-in to the discussion. But before he could explain, Veda asked, "Who planted these?" The poor petunias were drooping.

"My grandmother," Arthur said.

"I guess she's still gone," Veda said.

Arthur nodded.

"They don't look so good," Veda said. "What if we water them right now?"

Veda was responsible this way.

"I guess?"

Before he could bring up the grave, Veda was on her way back across the parking lot, was grabbing the hose rolled up on a spool by the Employees Only door, was dragging the hose toward the thirsty flowers.

"I bet the plants are grateful," Veda said several minutes later as they watched the water run.

"Can plants *be* grateful?" Arthur asked, thinking the question was like the one he still had about rodents and souls.

"Yes," Veda said. "Now what do you want to talk to me about?"

Glad to be back on track, Arthur pointed at the Popsicle-stick cross. "See that?"

Veda understood right away. "Something died?"

"It was Ramona's mouse," Arthur said.

"I didn't know she had a mouse," Veda said.

Arthur nodded. "She did. But now I—"

"The niños had hamsters for a while," Veda interrupted. "Do you think that's enough water?" The dampened earth smelled sweet and—was Arthur imagining it?—the flowers stood a bit straighter.

"Probably enough," Arthur said. "We're running out of time to walk." Together he and Veda dragged the hose back, shut off the faucet, rolled the hose up on its spool again.

"So, about Ramona's mouse," Arthur began as they set out toward the trail.

"Did Ramona love it a lot?" Veda asked.

Arthur thought about that. "I don't know. When it died, she asked for a puppy."

"The niños' hamsters gave me the creeps," Veda said. "Mom says puppies make a mess."

By this time they were on the dirt trail. It was narrow, and they walked single file, Veda in front. Arthur had begun to feel annoyed. "So I guess you don't want to hear about the mouse," he said.

"I never said that. I'm your friend, Arthur. Listening is the job of a friend." Veda looked back.

Arthur agreed and opened his mouth to tell her that Mouse 4 was now a ghost, but she interrupted.

"Like, for example, I've been kind of wanting to talk to somebody about Juan," she said.

"What about Juan?" Arthur asked.

"But if you want to talk to me about a *mouse*—"

"No, it's okay. What about Juan?" Arthur repeated. "Do you not like him? Or—"

"He's been working for my mom. As a house cleaner, you know. I don't know if that is such a good idea. What do we know about him really? What if he's a thief or something? Mom's cleaners go into people's houses. Stuff is lying around sometimes. Valuable stuff. It's important that they don't take anything. If they do, Mom could lose her business."

Arthur thought of Randolph, how Officer Bernstein had suspected that he'd stolen that ring. "But why do you think Juan's dishonest?"

"He's too handsome," Veda said.

"Wait . . . *what*?" Arthur smiled. "I thought girls . . . women . . . females, whatever, I thought they liked handsome."

"And he has so many tattoos," Veda said.

"Half the world has tattoos, Veda. Even Mrs. Danneberg. Did you notice? It's on her arm, a cartoon lady saying 'Shhhh!'?"

"Juan's tattoos do not say 'Shhhh.' They're more usual:

skulls and flowers and cars." Veda pulled her phone out of the pocket of her shorts, looked at the time. "Should we turn around?"

Arthur nodded. "Probably, yeah." They were less than halfway around the lake; they had to be back in twenty minutes. They stopped for a moment, and Arthur looked up. Far above them a paraglider flew. This wasn't unusual. There was a launching platform in the hills right above them.

Arthur thought the paragliders were crazy. Who would want to jump off a cliff?

On the other hand paragliders weren't ordinary, didn't stick to the comfortable and the familiar. Paragliders were adventurous.

He and Veda turned around.

"Can't you let your mom worry about whether Juan is honest?" Arthur said. "She hires people all the time. I bet she knows what she's doing."

"Yeah, usually," Veda agreed. "But I'm afraid that with Juan she might be making a mistake. You know, her brain might not be working right? All because she *likes* him."

"*Ewww,*" Arthur said. He was walking more slowly than Veda, looking out for prairie dogs and rabbits. Now she stopped to wait for him. The path was wider at this point, and they continued walking side by side.

"What did you want to talk to me about again? Ramona's dead mouse?" she asked.

They were almost back by now. The conversation hadn't gone the way he'd planned, and all of a sudden he felt shy. Veda was his best friend, but she had her own stuff to worry about. If Arthur told her about Watson, Veda might think he'd gone crazy—her best friend had gone crazy. Then she'd have even more to worry about.

But he had to tell her something. He had asked her to come to work early, straight from swimming. So he said the first thing that came into his head. "Last week after you left? This teacup showed up out of nowhere in Fine China. And it's like a mystery. I mean, someone stole it from my grandma a long time ago. And now it's back."

"Crazy," Veda said. "Where is it now?"

"In my room," Arthur said.

"Seriously?" Veda said. "Why do *you* want it?"

Maybe he *should* tell her about Watson?

Why, all of a sudden, did everything in life seem complicated?

But it was too late. They were back at the store. For

an hour they sat at the big oak table, adding kitchen utensils and miscellaneous small household items to the UUI. Luckily, there wasn't too much merchandise that day, and they got done early.

"Can I see the teacup?" Veda asked Arthur.

"Sure," Arthur said. "But why?"

"I don't know. Because it's a mystery, I guess. Maybe you've missed a clue, Arthur."

Arthur thought of the way Veda had watered the flowers before. That was how she was, saw something to do and did it. If she decided to investigate something, she would get right to work.

Upstairs Veda inspected the teacup. "No clues," she announced. "I was hoping for maybe a fingerprint or something. But I like the dancing bear."

Arthur decided to try again. "So the other thing about the teacup," he said, "is, uh . . . remember how I told you about Ramona's mouse?"

Veda nodded.

"So, that mouse, I renamed her Watson because she—"

"Hi, Darth!" Ramona and her friend Edie were standing in the doorway.

"Hey, Mo." Veda turned toward Ramona. "Oh—and

your name's Edie, right? How are you guys? How's soccer?"

And then they were yakking, and then it was time for Veda to go, and Arthur had no more chances to explain about Watson. Maybe it was for the best? Arthur couldn't decide.

CHAPTER TWENTY

The air is thin in Boulder, which is at almost six thousand feet elevation, and the power of the sun is strong. In the winter this meant the kids at Arthur's school could eat lunch outside comfortably as long as the sun was out. But this time of year it was much nicer to eat in the shade of the picnic pavilion. Arthur and his friends sat at the same table every day, the second one from the corner.

That day, Monday, Arthur blinked as he ducked into the shade of the pavilion. Zeke was already seated at their table.

"Hey," Arthur said, and sat as well, and began opening the brown bag that contained his lunch. Inside were an apple and an orange besides a turkey sandwich and Cheez-Its, which for some reason his parents would buy him even though they would never buy barbecue chips.

Mysteries of parents.

Meanwhile, Danh and Ethan came over. Ethan, as usual, had half a sandwich in his mouth before he'd even sat down, while Danh removed packed lunch items one at a time and inspected each as if it might be contaminated.

The lunch crowd was loud that day. A fourth-grade girl at the next table had a high-pitched laugh like a shriek, and Zeke had to almost shout to be heard when he looked at Arthur and said: "So hey, you got a fancy *teacup* now, huh? Hope you don't *break* it."

Arthur had been wondering whether to eat his orange or his sandwich first, didn't quite hear Zeke till Danh started laughing.

"Will there be tea parties now? Can I come?" Zeke continued.

"Arthur's got a teacup?" Ethan said through a mouth full of food. "How *sweet*! Are you gonna get some dolls, too? Play tea party?"

Arthur caught on at last, but his reaction was lame: "Wait. No. What are you . . . ? I don't—"

He got no further than that because Zeke had to tell Ethan and Danh about the teacup, which had pictures of teddy bears, and soon there was a teapot, too, and then a whole tea set.

Of the four of them, Danh was probably the smartest, and he ran with the story: "Tea sets are like what grandmas have. *Great*-grandmas."

"Grandma Arthur." Zeke looked him over. "It fits."

When Arthur thought about it later, he knew he should've ignored them. But at the time his reaction was to explain.

Huge mistake.

"It's only one teacup, and it's cool, actually," he said. "It's got one bear on it, and it's from that old band the HoneyJams, and the bear is, like, dancing and—"

"Oooh—*dancing bears*!" Zeke said.

"Are they wearing whatzitcalled, tutus? Are they ballet bears?" Ethan asked.

"Ballet teddy bears!" Zeke howled. "That just sounds so *cute*, doesn't it, Danny?"

"Very cute," Danh agreed.

"Tell us more, Grandma Art," Zeke said. "Pink ballet bears or what?"

Arthur retreated. "Shut up," he said, feeling miserable, and he took a bite of his sandwich, but it was hard to swallow, a lump in his throat.

"Ohhh, now we've hurt Grandma's feelings!" Ethan

said, and he and Danh and Zeke all laughed some more.

After that Arthur did shut up, ate his sandwich and tried to ignore the guys. But he felt the red heat on his face, felt trapped with them, with nowhere to look. Finally the subject changed—who was going to what camp when school was out, the Rockies game the day before, Danh's brother had a sweet new bike. Every time there was a pause, though, somebody would bring up the teacup and laugh, and Arthur would shrink some more.

Lunch ended after what seemed like a thousand years, and instead of walking to social studies with Danh like usual, Arthur went the long way, which gave him plenty of time to be mad, specifically mad at Veda for telling. Okay, sure, he hadn't exactly told her not to tell anybody about the teacup. But she should have known, right? A real friend would have known.

At least there was one lucky thing, though. He hadn't told Veda about Watson. He could only imagine what a disaster that would've been—if Zeke and the guys had heard about his friend the mouse.

Arthur didn't see Veda the rest of the day, which was lucky for Veda, but he did wonder how she'd happened to tell Zeke. Was it in homeroom? He knew she and Zeke had homeroom together with Mr. Racker. Had she told anybody else? Did he have to worry that any second somebody else would give him grief for owning a teddy bear teacup?

CHAPTER TWENTY-ONE

Arthur was too busy with customers to worry about friends or social status that afternoon at the store. In fact, lately the store had been so busy that Ramona had to help out. She was too short to stand behind the counter, but she knew where everything was, and she could direct the customers.

Usually Dad handled sales of CDs, sound equipment, and musical instruments. Those were things he knew a lot about. But that afternoon Dad was busy in the office, and Arthur was helping a teenage girl who was interested in buying a ukulele. From where he stood in Musical Instruments, Arthur saw the door to the office open and a guy come out. He had probably been talking to Dad about a job. Jennifer Y was gone a lot with the training for her race, and Grandpa had been sick. Dad was hoping to hire a couple of new clerks.

The guy from the office was parent-aged or a little

younger, Latino it looked like, handsome with a neat hair-cut. He was wearing a pale blue polo, so Arthur could see the tattoo sleeves on his arms. Suddenly Arthur suspected he knew exactly who this was, and he might've said hello, but his customer had questions: Was Kala really the best ukulele? How about this Pomaikai?

Arthur answered the questions, showed off a few more ukuleles. Finally the girl said she had to think it over and left. Arthur was afraid he might've talked too much, but he didn't have time to worry long. Soon he had to help a woman with designer purses. She was wearing a black hoodie with a gold buffalo, the University of Colorado mascot, and Arthur figured she was a student.

"I don't see," the student said, examining a bag with a French label, "how your store can claim to be 'saving the earth' when you're selling *leather*! Don't you know a living creature *died* to make this purse?"

Arthur nodded thoughtfully. "On the other hand," he said, "it's a vintage purse. So the creature died a long time ago."

This argument seemed to convince the student, because she bought the purse. "Enjoy your purchase," he said, "and thank you for shopping at Universal Trash."

Next, Ramona came up to the counter leading an older white man who was wearing a tweed jacket and beat-up jeans. He had gray hair, which needed to be combed, and a wrinkled face. Grandpa would've called him an old hippie, and Arthur sussed out he might be a professor.

"May I help you, sir?" Arthur asked.

Ramona answered. "He is looking for a watch. I told him you have the key to the jewelry case."

"Thank you, miss," the man said. Either he didn't mind being helped by a person who was not quite seven years old, or he hadn't noticed. Dad said some professors were like that, "kind of oblivious."

Arthur grabbed the key, which was on a ring with three others, each labeled with tape in his grandfather's tiny handwriting. "We have a fine selection of timepieces," he said, "many of them antiques."

"All watches are antiques these days, wouldn't you say?" The man smiled. "Unless they make toast."

Were there watches that made toast? Or was the man making a joke?

The man smiled. "What I mean is that many of today's timepieces do much more than keep time. But I thought it might be nice to go old-school, have something simple that

I consult only for hours and minutes, not the weather, my blood pressure, and the definition of 'parallax.'"

Professor for sure, Arthur thought.

The glass jewelry case to the right of the cash counter was about Arthur's height. Now he directed the professor's attention. "Most of the watches are on this shelf. I'm happy to get one out for you if you'd like."

"I like the looks of that one there," the man said after a minute. "Reminds me of my uncle. He was a stylish gentleman. Always wore a hat, and I don't mean a ball cap, either."

Arthur twisted the key in the small silver lock, pulled open the glass door, reached in, and retrieved a round gold watch, maybe two inches in diameter, set in a black velvet box. Even before he held the watch, he could tell it would be heavy, which probably meant expensive. He wondered if this man might actually buy it, or if he was taking a look for fun, or if he'd see the price sticker—$895—and hand the watch right back. Grandpa had taught Arthur that you never knew with customers. The ones who looked prosperous might be penniless, and the ones who looked hungry had a wallet full of hundred-dollar bills.

"That's why it pays to be nice to all of them," Grandpa said—or used to say before he started feeling free to express so many opinions.

"Tiffany." The man read the brand name printed on the watch face, then took the watch out of its box. "Oh and look here, it's engraved. What unusual initials!" He turned the watch over and showed Arthur the ornate letters etched on the back.

"XYZ," Arthur read.

The Y in the middle—the largest of the three—stood for the last name, Arthur knew. The X would be the first name, and Z the middle name.

"I don't think I know any names that start with X," Arthur said.

"'Xavier'?" the man said, and spelled it out. "Not a common name around here. Still, you have to wonder who the owner was. He's dead now, I expect."

Arthur nodded. "It may have come from an estate. I can look it up if you want."

The man placed the watch back into the box, and Arthur thought he'd say thanks, he'd think about it. But the man surprised him. "I'll take it," he said.

All cool, Arthur nodded like that was just what he'd

expected. "Excellent choice. I'm sure there's not another like it in all of Boulder, maybe all of Colorado."

The man laughed.

Arthur took the watch, moved over to the cash counter, pulled out the pad of blank receipts. "We take cash, checks with proper ID, and all major credit cards," he said.

"Checks?" the man said. "Almost no one takes checks anymore."

"We like to provide as many options as possible for our customers," Arthur said.

The man pulled out his wallet, inserted a credit card into the reader. Arthur felt a moment of worry. This was a big purchase, one of the biggest Arthur had ever rung up, and sometimes there was a problem with the credit going through, which could be embarrassing.

While the machine and the bank talked to each other, the man said, "Actually, would you mind telling me who brought it in? Since it's about to be mine, I'm curious."

"Okay." Arthur nodded, but when he looked at the ID number from the price tag—021523DJ—he had to apologize. Arthur could see that the watch had come in on February 15 of the current year, and that his dad had logged it. But instead of a name on the third line to indicate the provenance, who had brought it in, there was the word "Red." "Oh, sorry," Arthur said. "This one's from the Red File. I can't give out the information."

"The Red File?" The man widened his eyes. "How intriguing!"

The credit charge went through. Arthur looked at the screen, saw that the man's name was Phineas Worth— professor for sure!—and wrote up the receipt. "Some of our consigners don't want their names given out," he explained. "We keep the record in case there's a problem, but it's in what we call the Red File."

"A problem?" Mr. Worth repeated. "Like the item turns out to be stolen?"

"That's extremely rare," Arthur said, which was true and also how his dad had instructed all the clerks to answer that question. "We know many of our consigners personally. At the same time, we keep very good records." Arthur handed over the bag. "I'm sure you'll enjoy your watch, Mr. Worth. Thank you for shopping at Universal Trash."

CHAPTER TWENTY-TWO

That evening Arthur helped his dad make dinner. It was better than doing homework, better than thinking about Zeke and the lunch table, better than thinking how mad he was at Veda.

"Get the noodle pot out for me," Dad said, stifling a yawn. "I'm making spaghetti."

Arthur did as directed, and Dad filled the pot with water.

"I am beat," Dad said. "I wish your grandmother were back. We could use her help in the store."

Arthur missed his grandmother too. She was the one he used to tell about stuff that happened at school, stuff with friends or people he thought were friends. He hadn't done that in a while. He was too old, wasn't he?

"When is she supposed to come home?" he asked.

Dad was chopping onions, and the raw smell filled the kitchen. "Your mom thinks she'll be back by the weekend," he said. "Her book group meeting is coming up. I guess that's more important than the store to her. I wish I could put her on the schedule for Saturday. Jennifer Y has that race, and the new guy wasn't sure he'd be able to start that soon."

"New guy" made Arthur remember the man in the polo shirt. "Oh yeah," he said. "Was that Juan, Veda's mom's friend? Did you hire him?"

"Juan." Dad nodded. "I still have to check references, but I'm sure if he's good enough for Maria, he's good enough for us."

"Does he work for Maria?" Arthur said. "Or . . . ?"

"Works for her, yes," Dad said. "I'm not sure about the 'or' part. So I guess Veda has mentioned him?"

Arthur thought of saying that Veda didn't like him, but that didn't seem fair. Anyway, now Arthur would meet him and get to decide for himself.

"She thinks he's funny," Arthur said.

Dad poured oil into the frying pan. "Funny's good," he said. "You gotta have a sense of humor to work at the store, right? To deal with Grandpa for sure. Can you set the table, please, Arthur? I mean, you've been a *huge* help already, but . . ."

"Funny, Dad," Arthur said. Then he set the table.

• • •

Watson appeared on the bedpost as usual that night. Of course, the first thing she did was ask Arthur about the teacup. "Have you made progress with my mystery?" she wanted to know.

Thinking of the teacup made Arthur think of Veda blabbing, so he told Watson what had happened at lunch. While he talked, he felt his stomach tensing up.

"I guess I don't understand humans," Watson said, giving her nose a good rub with her paws. "Why do your friends care that you own a teacup? Would they make fun of me for hanging out in a teacup?"

That was an easy question, and Arthur said, "No." But why they cared that he owned a teacup was harder to explain. He didn't want to say "because teacups are girly." Watson was a girl, and that might sound insulting, even if he, Arthur, didn't think a teacup was girly, and he, Arthur, didn't think being girly was bad either.

Did his friends think being girly was bad? Arthur wasn't sure. But they did think being girly was wrong for a dude. Arthur didn't think he agreed with that either, but it was a lot to explain, especially to a mouse. And what if after that Watson told Arthur that the solution was new friends?

"New friends don't grow on trees, you know," Arthur said out loud.

"What's that?" Watson asked. "Trees?"

Arthur realized he'd been arguing with his own thoughts. "Sorry," he said. "Uh, so why they care is that none of them has a teacup, I guess. So it's unusual. And unusual is, like, weird, and those guys think if it's weird, it's bad. Does that make sense?"

Watson's nose bobbed up and down, her version of nodding. "With mice," she said, "it's the same thing. Disagreement is bad for the colony, so everyone in the colony has to have the same tastes and opinions. No weirdos allowed. I didn't know humans were so much like mice."

"Wait, you live in a colony?" Arthur said.

"Well, not anymore," Watson said, "obviously."

"Do you miss your colony?" Arthur was thinking that even though family and friends were a pain, he wouldn't like to live without them.

"I don't," Watson said. "I guess it's like food. There are certain things you need in life that you don't need when you're a ghost. What if you tell your friends you smashed the teacup?"

Sometimes Arthur had a hard time following Watson's conversation. "Wait . . . what?"

"That would make them happy, right? Convince them you were tough, not the type to own a teacup, not unusual. Only, don't actually smash it, because I like it, okay?"

Arthur wrinkled his nose. "You mean I should lie?"

"Why not?" Watson said.

"Because lying is wrong?" Arthur said, at the same time thinking that he was bad at lying and he might get caught.

"Look at it this way," Watson said. "What's more important, having friends or telling a lie?"

This question was too hard for a sleepy person. "I'll see you tomorrow, okay, Watson?"

"Sweet dreams," Watson said.

CHAPTER TWENTY-THREE

A sixth grader who was not Arthur Popper might have found Veda before school the next morning and told her flat out, "You blabbed about my teacup and I got razzed by the guys at lunch, and that hurt my feelings, and it's your fault, and I'm mad at you."

Arthur Popper did not do that. Arthur Popper did not like confrontation. Confrontation made him anxious. So Arthur Popper decided to avoid the issue, which meant avoiding Veda.

This was tricky that day, Tuesday, because he and Veda had library together, but he accomplished it by asking Mrs. Danneberg to help him find a book.

Mrs. Danneberg was delighted. "How about one of the King Arthur legends?" She suggested several, which Arthur rejected. Some of them had sounded interesting, but to stay away from Veda, he wanted to keep Mrs. Danneberg talking.

"Are there other legends besides King Arthur?" he asked.

Well, yes, there certainly were! Mrs. Danneberg suggested stories from ancient Greece and ancient Rome and even fairy tales, which were close relatives of legends, but Arthur rejected every one until the period neared its end.

"Actually, I guess *The Legend of King Arthur* would be okay," he said at last.

He knew he was being a pain and expected Mrs. Danneberg to roll her eyes. But instead she sighed and said, "*Good*. Next week you can let me know how you liked it."

Library was third period. Then came fourth period, then lunch. About midway through fourth period, math, Arthur felt his stomach tighten. He was worried about what would happen at lunch. Should he sit at the usual table? Sit by himself? Sit with other people he knew?

He knew other people, right? Well, yeah. But they were not people he sat with at lunch.

When the time came, habit won out, and he walked to the usual table. He was the first that day. As he unpacked his lunch, the other guys arrived and he grunted at them, but hardly looked up, expecting Teacup II, the Sequel.

And if that happened, if they teased him again, would

he follow Watson's questionable advice and claim he had smashed it?

He didn't think so.

And anyway the teacup didn't come up.

The guys acted normal, talked about other stuff, and finally he joined in.

Were they over it?

Maybe. But even when lunch ended, Arthur couldn't be sure. The teacup could show up as a topic anytime. He had to stay alert.

By the time school ended, Arthur was tired. Maybe he was staying up too late getting bad advice from Watson? Sitting on the bus, he wished he could take a nap or play *Mario Kart* when he got home, but he couldn't because Dad needed him at the store.

Again.

Arthur was looking forward to time off after Dad hired Juan and his grandmother returned. Grandma would be back before Monday, Arthur knew, because that's when her book group met. How did he know that? Because Mom was freaking out, same as every month: she hadn't started the book yet.

Arthur thought of mentioning to Mom that the book was sort of like homework, and she was always telling him to get a jump on homework, not do it at the last minute.

But he decided not to.

Arthur walked into the store, heard the entrance bell chime, saw half a dozen customers poking around Dining Room Furniture, Housewares, Lighting, and Wildlife—departments close to the entrance.

Half a dozen was a lot for a Tuesday. No hope of a nap now.

"Hey, there's the kid of the hour." Arthur's dad waved at him from Floral. With Dad was Juan, dressed, again, in a polo shirt. Arthur tried not to stare at the tattoos. "Have you two met?" Dad looked from one to the other.

"Not yet," Juan said. "You're Veda's friend, right?"

Juan probably had not intended for that question to be difficult, but it was. Arthur was still mad at Veda, hadn't spoken to her all day. Still, he didn't hate her. So were they friends?

Arthur's answer was a smile and an elbow bump, which Juan returned.

"I'm showing the new guy around," Arthur's dad said. "Training him, that is. He's a quick study. By tomorrow he'll be on the floor helping out. I was just about to show him the UUI."

"I never worked anyplace without a computer before," Juan said. "Maria uses a spreadsheet for scheduling cleaners and budgeting, too."

"Are you going to keep working for her?" Dad asked.

"Claro—for sure," Juan said. "It's a good gig, actually. Maria appreciates it when you do a good job."

"We do too," Dad said. "And about the computer . . . well, Byron likes his old index-card system, and frankly it's not worth fighting him."

"Byron's your . . . father?" Juan asked.

"Wife's father," Dad said. "And founder of the store way back when, along with his wife, Linda. They're Arthur's grandparents."

Juan nodded. "Good to know the history."

"Excuse me?" A mom-aged woman with long red hair came up to the three of them. "I'm looking for a sweatshirt for my son? He's five. Preferably red? Preferably no Disney? Can you point me . . . ?"

Arthur said, "Happy to help, ma'am," nodded to Juan, and proceeded to show the woman every small red sweatshirt in the store.

None was exactly right, so he showed her every small orange sweatshirt too. Finally she found a blue one herself. The picture on the front was Pluto, a Disney character, but she declared that Pluto was okay because he was an *original* Disney character.

"I totally see what you mean," Arthur said. "Can I help you find anything else? We have an excellent selection of toys, for example."

"No, no," the red-haired woman said. "We should be bringing *you* toys. Half the ones my son has? He never plays with them."

"I can ring you up, then," Arthur said.

Grandpa had come out of the office while Arthur was finding sweatshirts. Now, as Arthur crossed the store, he saw Grandpa, his dad, and Juan standing in Electronics talking. Arthur couldn't hear what they were saying.

At the cash counter the woman set down the cloth bag she'd been carrying, untangled the straps of her purse, unzipped her purse, pulled out her wallet and credit card. Arthur noticed there was a book in the bag—*Of Mice and Men*. Was she also in his mom's book group?

The woman's name was Molly Hart. Arthur saw it on the credit card as he wrote up the receipt. At the same time, he noticed that Grandpa had raised his voice.

Uh-oh.

Meanwhile Molly Hart peered into the jewelry case.

"I'd be happy to show you anything that's of interest, ma'am." Arthur spoke a little louder than usual.

"Oh no." Molly Hart smiled and shook her head. "I was just thinking I'm as bad as my son—only instead of toys, I have jewelry. That gold bracelet?" She pointed. "My aunt gave me one like it. For graduation maybe? It's pretty, but I don't wear bracelets. It just sits around in my jewelry box."

The words seemed familiar to Arthur, but before he could think, Grandpa's volume level rose again: "All I'm saying is, you have to be extra careful when you hire certain kinds of people. What's the matter with that?"

Dad's voice was almost as loud: "Take it easy, Byron. Juan, I'm sorry. Let me assure you that this attitude does *not* represent mine or the business's either. We couldn't be happier to have you—"

"What do you mean my attitude doesn't represent the business?" Grandpa was not taking it easy. "I *am* the business, in case you've forgotten. And if I say we have to be careful who we hire, then we have to be careful who we hire."

Embarrassed, Arthur felt his face turn red. "Uh . . . my grandfather," he said to Molly Hart, who was staring.

"I know your mom, I think," Molly Hart said quietly, "and your grandmother, too. We belong—"

Now it was Juan's voice that interrupted: "I don't need any job enough to put up with this."

"I'll just take my son's new sweatshirt." Molly Hart reached across the counter.

"Oh! Sorry." Arthur handed over the sweatshirt. "Thank you for shopping at Universal Trash."

Ms. Hart managed a sympathetic half smile before she turned to go.

Arthur wanted to see what was going on without being seen himself, so he sneaked into Fine China, then peered through a jungle of silk flowers and plastic leaves. Juan, he saw right away, was gone—headed for the exit.

"What did I tell you, Dan?" Grandpa said to Arthur's dad. "They don't really want to work."

CHAPTER TWENTY-FOUR

A voice piped up from behind Arthur's right shoulder: "Shameful, just shameful. I heard the whole thing. I don't see how Linda puts up with him."

Arthur turned his head and saw Mrs. Merdle. She was the grandmother of Ramona's friend Edie, besides being the prairie dog authority who visited second-grade classes. And she had known Arthur's grandmother for a long time.

Arthur said, "Hi, Mrs. Merdle."

"How can *you* stand it, Arthur?" she went on.

Arthur didn't know what to say except, "He's my grandfather."

Mrs. Merdle was only an inch taller than Arthur and wiry. Short gray hair framed her sun-wrinkled face. She was wearing her prairie dog earrings, a HoneyJams T-shirt, running tights, and sneakers.

"Well, he isn't my grandfather," she said. "If I didn't

have a Stomp meeting, I'd tell him what I thought."

"A Stomp meeting?" Arthur said.

Mrs. Merdle looked at her watch. "In twenty minutes. You know what Stomp is, Arthur. Fundraiser for prairie dog habitat? Your parents go every year."

"Oh, sure," Arthur said. "The Stomp part is dancing. Uh . . . I think my dad is steering Grandpa toward the office."

"Get him out of the way," Mrs. Merdle said, her eyes fierce. But when she looked at Arthur, they softened. "How are you, anyway? Seems like you're working all the time."

"Lots of new customers lately," Arthur said.

"Yes?" Mrs. Merdle seemed interested. "What kind of new customers?"

"Uh, you know, people who maybe wouldn't have shopped in a store like ours, shopped for used stuff," Arthur said. "But now they're trying to be more green, same as our ads say."

"Really," said Mrs. Merdle, then, "Oh! Why, hello, Molly. How nice to see you."

Arthur saw that Ms. Hart hadn't left.

"Oh, hello, Amy," Ms. Hart said. "So you shop here too? It's much nicer than I expected, and such excellent customer service." She smiled at Arthur, then held up a picture frame. "I was on my way out when I spotted this. Everett—he's the five-year-old—got a photo with the Easter Bunny. This will be just right."

"Happy to ring you up," Arthur said. "Or do you want to look around some more?"

"No, no. This will be it. I promise," Ms. Hart said. "Have you finished the book yet?" she asked Mrs. Merdle. "It's good but so sad."

"Not yet," Mrs. Merdle said. "I'm awfully busy with Stomp. I'm so glad you and your husband are attending."

"Wouldn't miss it," Molly Hart said.

Arthur expected Mrs. Merdle to head for the exit after that, but she changed her mind. "I think I *will* have a little talk with your grandpa," she said. "I have time if I keep it short."

Arthur never heard what happened between Mrs. Merdle and Grandpa in the office. The ceiling didn't cave in, though. The windows did not blow out. Like a lot of people, Mrs. Merdle had a bag slung over her shoulder, and when she came out, something was bouncing around inside.

Maybe it's her copy of the book for book group, Arthur thought, and he would've told her goodbye, but he was helping still another kid with a ukulele. *What is up with ukuleles?* he wondered. Some new Hawaii show he never heard of? This was the kind of thing he'd know if his parents let him have more screen time. Really, it was no wonder Zeke and Ethan and Danh thought he was weird. It wasn't his fault. It was his parents'.

That night at bedtime Arthur told Watson how Grandpa had offended Juan and Juan had left.

"Slow down a little, Arthur," Watson said. "I'm not sure I understand. What did your grandpa say that was bad?"

Arthur was glad it was dark in his room. Just remembering, he could feel his face burn. "He said you have to be careful hiring 'certain kinds of people.' Then he made it worse. He said 'some people' don't like to work. He meant people like Juan, and Juan is Latino. It was an insulting thing to say, and besides—obviously—it's not even true."

Watson twitched her whiskers. "Bad, very bad. Can your grandpa change, do you think?"

"You're the wise one, Watson. Can old people change?"

"I don't know about people," Watson said. "But old rodents do get stubborn."

The idea of Grandpa as an old rodent made Arthur smile, and smiling made him feel better—but not for long. He told the part where after dinner his dad had called Juan and apologized again, and Juan had been polite but still said no to the job.

"You should talk to Veda about this," Watson said.

Without thinking, Arthur said, "No way," then, "She blabbed on me." Then, when Watson didn't reply, *"Why do I have to talk to her?"*

"Because someone in your family offended her mom's friend," Watson said.

"The weird part is Grandpa likes Veda," Arthur said. "He doesn't call Veda 'certain kinds of people.'"

"Your grandfather might not be . . . making total sense?" Watson said.

Arthur sighed. "Everything is officially terrible. But maybe when Grandma gets back, she can sort it out. Maybe if Grandpa says sorry to Juan. But I don't think he . . ." Arthur's words dissolved into a yawn.

"You have to talk to Veda," Watson repeated, "and solve the mystery of my teacup too."

CHAPTER TWENTY-FIVE

I t wasn't that Arthur disagreed with Watson exactly.

He knew he'd eventually have to talk to Veda. He was still mad at her, but they worked together on Sunday afternoons. They couldn't work together without talking.

He also wanted to solve the mystery. The best way to start would be to question Grandpa B. Where was the teacup the last time he saw it? Were any shady characters around then, potential teacup thieves?

But Arthur didn't want to talk to his grandfather. He was mad at him, too, same as everyone else was. And besides, would Grandpa B really remember any details after all this time?

So Arthur felt stuck.

At school, Wednesday, Thursday, and Friday passed without Ethan, Danh, or Zeke mentioning the teacup. Maybe they had forgotten?

And Veda was surprisingly easy to avoid. He didn't talk to her at all.

After school on Friday, Arthur worked at the store. First he helped a guy find kitchen gadgets: a grater, a peeler, two paring knives. Then he showed a woman an assortment of footstools, but she was fussy, and none was the right color for her den. It was almost six o'clock when he saw Jennifer Y getting ready to leave. Her race was this weekend, and he wished her good luck.

"You're really going to run a hundred miles on a trail?" he said, and then, he couldn't help it: "Why?"

Jennifer Y grinned. "Makes me happy. Makes me feel alive."

Arthur said, "Alive is good," but then he thought of Watson, who didn't seem to mind being dead. "I mean, I guess."

"You should try running," Jennifer said. "Just see if you like it. When I was your age, I couldn't run a hundred yards."

Arthur knew he could run a hundred yards. They had to run more than that for PE. But could he run a whole mile? Thinking of Officer Bernstein, he calculated: a mile was 1 percent of what Jennifer was going to run that weekend.

"You really couldn't?" Arthur said.

"Nope," Jennifer said. "But one day I was sad about something, never mind what, but it had to do with a *B-O-Y*, and I thought running would help distract my head, and I was right, and—I'm skipping some stuff—basically, I got hooked."

Arthur said he'd think about it, and then he said good luck again, and then Jennifer left. Would she be back to work on Monday? Even if she didn't trip and fall off a mountain, she was bound to be all blistered and in pain.

He was staring after her, thinking these grim thoughts, when he heard a horsepower roar, then *puh-puh-puh-putt*, then quiet.

Arthur didn't want to get his hopes up, but he went to the door and looked out into the parking lot.

There, in a spot marked NO PARKING, was a red motorcycle—a Triumph Bonneville T100. Astride it, a thin figure in black leathers removed gloves, unclipped chin strap, and tugged off helmet to reveal . . .

"Grandma!" Arthur cried, and pushed open the door.

"Tell me you didn't grow any more, Arthur," Grandma said as she squeezed him. "You're bigger than I am, I think, and I don't like it."

"I'm really glad you're back, Grandma," Arthur said, but since he was speaking into her shoulder, his words were squished.

Arthur's grandmother was tall—his father called her "stately"—with a wide mouth and gray eyes. Her hair, now helmet-flattened, was gray too, even if she insisted it was silver. Her idea of makeup was a messy smear of lip balm. Now she pushed Arthur arm's-length away so she could look into his face. "What was that? My skull's still buzzing from the road."

"I'm glad you're back," he repeated.

Grandma cocked her head and frowned. "Glad, or relieved? How has your grandpa been?"

Arthur was glad his dad came out at that moment so he didn't have to answer.

"Linda!" Dad said. "Boy, am I glad to see you!"

"Uh-oh." Grandma tugged a handful of her hair. "Where is he?"

"Grandma's back!" Arthur told Watson at bedtime. Then he explained how she'd arrived on her motorcycle, checked in with everyone in Arthur's family, given them all hugs, and hurried back to her house to see Grandpa.

Watson rubbed her nose and whiskers. "Don't she and Grandpa talk while she's on one of her trips? Haven't they ever heard of texting?"

"I don't know," Arthur said. "I don't understand grown-ups."

"Anyway," Watson went on, "now you can ask your grandmother about the teacup. You can start detecting!"

"You're right," Arthur said. "And I will. I swear."

"And don't forget Veda," Watson said.

"Has anyone ever told you you're bossy?" Arthur asked.

"What you call 'bossy,' I call 'helpful,'" Watson said.

Arthur admitted he wasn't that mad at Veda anymore. He even missed her a little. "I'll call her tomorrow," he said. "I bet she misses me too."

CHAPTER TWENTY-SIX

After breakfast the next morning Arthur went back to his room, sat on the edge of his bed, took a deep breath, pulled out his phone, tapped Veda's name and waited for her to answer. When she didn't right away, he almost hung up, felt relief, actually, but then her voice came on, "Bueno?"

"Hi," Arthur said. "Uh . . . are you—?"

He was going to say "busy," but there was a *bump* like the phone had fallen and then the sound of footsteps and kids laughing, and Veda in the distance yelling, "Dale eso ahora!" which even Arthur could translate: "Give that back!"

Finally, after a bunch more *bump-thump*s and some squealing, Veda said, "Arthur? Sorry. What's up?"

"I didn't mean to bother you," Arthur said.

"Cállate!" Veda said. "Not you, Arthur. Mom's working. I've got the niños till noon. I might murder them

before that, though. No, you can't have biscochos! What did Mamá say?"

Arthur didn't know what Mamá had said, but he figured it must've had something to do with biscochos. "I called to say I'm sorry," Arthur said. "About my grandpa, I mean. Did Juan tell you? Or your mom? And I'm also sorry, kind of, that I stopped speaking to you. I mean, now I want to stay speaking to you."

There. Having worked up the courage to call, Arthur had gotten all the words out fast.

"Wait. . . . Okay," Veda said. Arthur heard what sounded like a door closing, and it got quiet. "I've shut myself in my mom's room. But I can't talk for very long 'cause they'll do damage. I know about Juan, yeah."

"I'm sorry," Arthur said again. "I don't . . . I mean . . . My grandpa isn't me."

"Yeah. It's still bad, though, what he said—'those people.'"

Arthur took a breath. "I know. I'm sorry. I don't know what else to say. He's still my grandfather. And anyway, you can still help out on Sundays, right? Tomorrow?"

"Maybe not tomorrow. Maybe next week," Veda said.

Arthur felt terrible. His reflex was to say "sorry" again,

but "sorry" wasn't helping. For a second it was quiet.

Then Veda said, "I'd better check on the niños."

"No, wait," Arthur said. "Why did you tell everybody about the teacup? Zeke, I mean."

"Teacup?" Veda repeated. "What are you talking about?"

"That's why I'm not speaking to you," Arthur clarified. "Because you told everybody, Zeke, about the teacup."

"You're not speaking to me?" Veda said.

"I am now, Veda. Duh. Obviously. But I wasn't. At school I mean. All week?"

There was a pause like Veda was thinking. Then she said, "Was the teacup a secret or something?"

"Not exactly," Arthur said.

"Then I don't get—" Veda began, but Arthur interrupted.

"Zeke razzed me about it. Like dudes aren't supposed to have teacups."

"Dudes can have teacups, Arthur," Veda said.

"But why would you *tell* him?" Arthur wasn't ready to let this go. If she could be mad at him about his grandpa, which wasn't really fair, if you thought about it, couldn't he be mad at her about something that was also not fair?

Veda said, "I don't know." Then, "Oh yeah. I guess I remember. We were talking about Mr. Racker's coffee mug? How it's cracked. How he never washes it. And I thought of the teacup because of the chip, and I said how you found it, how it was kind of mysterious. Anyway, I guess Zeke was there."

"Wait, you mean there were *other* people?" Arthur wondered who else was going to give him grief.

"It's not a big deal," Veda said. "Look, now it's all of a sudden quiet—the niños, I mean. I gotta go. I might see you tomorrow. I have to talk to my mom and maybe Juan. Oh, but wanna know something weird? They're at your grandparents' house this morning. Cleaning. Your grandma's having people over, and she wanted the house clean first."

"That is weird," Arthur said, "and awkward."

"I thought my mom would cancel," Veda said, "but she said your grandma was one of her first customers, and Juan was the only guy available—" A *crash* interrupted. "Oh *no*. Gotta go, Arthur."

Arthur wanted to say "Sorry" again or "Are we still friends?" or "Please come tomorrow," but before he could say anything, Veda was gone.

CHAPTER TWENTY-SEVEN

With Grandma back, Arthur didn't have to help out in the store that morning, but he went downstairs anyway. Luckily, it wasn't that busy yet, and the two of them sat in chairs by the big walnut dining table. Grandma told him that on her trip she'd traveled to Utah to see the sights: Zion, Bryce Canyon, Moab, the Great Salt Lake. The photos on her phone showed pink rock formations, blue sky, white clouds. The landscape was desert-y, almost no green at all.

"The colors are nice," Arthur said. "But I think I like trees."

"Me too," Grandma said. "But I hadn't been to Utah in a long time. Maybe the next trip will be to someplace with more water. Niagara Falls maybe. Or Chicago."

"Why don't you ever go anywhere with Grandpa?" Arthur asked. Maybe this was nosy, but if you couldn't be nosy to your own family, who could you be nosy to?

"Your grandfather"—Grandma hesitated—". . . has many fine qualities. But he does not enjoy travel. He likes his routine. On Saturday mornings, for example, he likes to go to Boxcar and get a twelve-ounce house blend with two packets of sugar and drink it at one of the tables on the sidewalk."

"And if his favorite table is taken, he gets annoyed," Arthur said.

Grandma nodded.

"Dad told you about the Juan thing, right? Did you talk to Grandpa about that?" Arthur asked.

Grandma sighed. "It didn't seem wise to bring it up first thing," she said. "But I'm glad he's out of the house while they clean. My book group is coming over on Monday, my turn to host."

"*Of Mice and Men,*" Arthur said.

Grandma's gray eyes got big. "What a detective you must be, Arthur. *How* did you know that?"

Arthur echoed Sherlock Holmes: "Elementary, my dear grandmother." Then he explained how a couple of customers had mentioned the book. "I'd like to be a detective," he added. "But I don't think I'm that brave. If I had to confront a criminal, I'd probably pass out."

Grandma said, "Dare to dream, Arthur. You can be whatever you want."

"No offense, but grown-ups always say that," Arthur said, "and for a fact, it isn't true. Dad wanted to be a musician. Mom's a lawyer, and she's grumpy all the time. What about you? What did you want to be?"

"A granny on a motorcycle," Grandma said.

That made Arthur laugh, and at the same time the entrance bell chimed to announce a customer. When Arthur turned, he saw the gentleman who'd bought the gold pocket watch.

Grandma stood up. "Welcome to Universal Trash. May I help you?"

"Good morning," the gentleman said. "Oh, and hello to you, young man. You'll be glad to know the watch is running fine."

"I am glad," Arthur said. "And good morning to you, Mr. Worth."

"Oh my." Mr. Worth's eyebrows shot up. "You remember my name!"

"He's good at customer service," said Grandma. "What can we help you with?"

"It's not shopping I'm after today," Mr. Worth

explained. "Instead I've got something to sell, consign, that is. If you're interested?"

"Usually my son-in-law handles consignments," Grandma said, "but he's busy in the office just now. What treasure have you brought us?"

Dad was almost always on the floor Saturday morning. What could he be busy with? Arthur decided to check, nodded goodbye to Grandma and Mr. Worth, headed for the office. On his way, he heard Mr. Worth explaining, "This just sits in my wife's jewelry box, so we thought why not—"

Arthur had to smile. There was a lot of jewelry "just sitting" in Boulder.

"Dad?" Arthur walked into the office but didn't see him. Instead he saw chaos—UUI boxes everywhere except where they belonged, neatly arranged on the shelves that lined the wall.

This was really weird. In Arthur's whole life he had never seen those shelves empty or the UUI moved all at once.

"Dad?" Arthur repeated.

"Right here—*ow*!" Dad's voice came from somewhere near the floor, and the *ow* had been preceded by a *bump*.

"Where?" Arthur closed the door, walked farther into the room, saw his dad's hindquarters poking out from under a desk. "Did you hit your head?" Arthur asked.

Arthur's dad skittered out, sat up, rubbed his head, frowned. "I did," he said, "and I didn't find the Red File either."

Arthur made a sympathy face. "Ouch. So . . . the Red File is missing?"

"I wouldn't be looking for it otherwise, would I?"

"Right," Arthur said. "I guess your head still hurts?"

Dad did not answer.

"Right," Arthur said again. "Do you want me to look for the Red File?"

Arthur's dad got to his feet and spread his hands to indicate the room. "Feel free. But you won't find it. I've looked everywhere."

CHAPTER TWENTY-EIGHT

Had someone taken the Red File? Why would they do that? For that matter, who even knew about the Red File? It wasn't a secret exactly, but it wasn't something they advertised either. Mostly who knew about it was the staff and the consigners whose names were in it, the ones who had brought in consignments they wanted to keep "confidential," which Arthur knew was a four-syllable word for "secret."

Since the shelves were empty, Arthur's dad decided to dust them, and Arthur said he'd help. Between sneezes, they talked.

"How did you happen to notice the Red File was missing?" Arthur asked. "Were you trying to put a new card in it?"

Dad shook his head. "I just saw there was a gap where it was supposed to be, like a missing tooth. It might've been gone for a while, though."

"I don't think a customer would've swiped it," Arthur said. "About the only people who come into the office are people who work here—and sometimes Officer Bernstein."

Dad looked thoughtful. "I did interview some potential new hires here," he said.

When the shelves were clean, Arthur and Dad returned each to its assigned spot. It had taken more than an hour, but the office looked normal again.

"It's like another mystery, isn't it?" Arthur said. "First the Found Teacup, now the Missing Red File. Grandma called me a detective just now, so maybe I should try to solve it."

"Isn't that what we're doing?" Dad said. "I mean, if movies and books are any guide, I'd say a detective does the same as us, asks questions and thinks logically. Oh, and I guess also looks for clues."

"Like if the thief left footprints or fingerprints or a bloody knife or whatever?" Arthur said.

"A bloody *knife*?" his dad repeated.

"Maybe we should call Officer Bernstein," Arthur said. "He's a professional."

"Not unless we find a knife," Dad said. "I doubt he cares about a file box. He'll just think I'm absentminded. I probably am absentminded. But that doesn't tell us where the file is."

The door to the office opened. Randolph leaned in. "Hey, Arthur. Hey, Boss. It's gettin' busy out there, uh-*huh*. Can you come and give us a hand?"

Dad nodded. "I'll be right there, but Arthur's supposedly got the morning off. Why don't you get outside or something, kiddo? I didn't mean to make you work all today. Air and sunshine. All that healthy stuff."

Arthur said he would. His dad smiled, but the smile was forced, and Arthur could tell he was still thinking about the Red File.

In the doorway Dad added, "Alternatively, feel free to scour the place for clues." And then he closed the door.

lone, Arthur did not exactly scour the place, but he did look around. No Red File. No bloody knife, either. Maybe plain thinking was a better strategy? Plain thinking he could do outside.

The day was typical for Boulder in May, and that meant clear and sunny. From the collection on hooks by the employee door, Arthur grabbed a Buffs ball cap, pulled it on, and headed across the parking lot toward his usual path. This was no time to try something new. He would need all available brainpower to think like a detective.

Thinking did not go well at first. There were so many distractions: The rocks and roots beneath his feet. The wild irises and bluebells. The prairie dogs, rabbits, and squirrels. The crows, ducks, nuthatches, and starlings. High above were those crazy paragliders, like giant insects on the breeze.

All of these demanded Arthur's attention, and dutifully

his brain pinged among them till suddenly (and to Arthur's surprise) it produced an actual, useful thought: someone might take the Red File because their name was in it, and they really, *really* did not want that known.

Because, for example, what they had consigned was stolen.

Another thought followed fast, maybe useful, for sure terrible: *What if that someone was Juan?*

Juan was one of the potential new hires Dad had interviewed in the office. He cleaned houses for Maria, and only the Sunday before, on this very same path, Veda had said her mom's clients sometimes left valuables lying around.

Could Juan have stolen something he found when he was cleaning houses? And could he have brought whatever it was, like a piece of jewelry, to the store to sell?

Arthur felt a pang. *Am I as bad as my grandpa?* he wondered. *Would I think the same stuff if Juan were Anglo, or if he didn't have so many tattoos?* He remembered something else Veda had said, how Juan was too handsome.

Too brown. Too tattooed. Too handsome.

People could be unfair about a lot of stuff.

But I'm *not unfair, am I?* Arthur thought. *I want to be better than that.*

Brain still busy, Arthur came in from his walk, made himself a PBJ, ate it standing up, wiped his lips with a paper towel, and went back downstairs to the store. He had a question for his dad, and he thought he'd see if his grandmother needed a break too. He could put off homework and reading *The Legend of King Arthur*.

He found his dad in the office, standing alone among the desks, hands on his hips, looking at the shelves that held the UUI.

"I didn't find a bloody knife," Arthur said.

"Bloody knife?" Dad looked alarmed, then said, "Oh, right. No, I didn't think you would, or any other clues, either. And no matter how hard I stare at the shelf, the Red File doesn't reappear."

"Bummer," Arthur said. "Can I ask you something real quick? You already knew Juan when he interviewed, right?"

Dad nodded. "I'd met him. I don't know if you'd say I knew him exactly. But he had great references. I mean, Maria is about as good as it gets."

Arthur didn't want to ask this next part. He worried he really would sound like his grandpa. At the same time, it was the job of detectives to ask questions.

"Did Juan ever bring anything in to consign?" Arthur asked. "Is his name in the Red File?"

"Come on, kiddo," Dad said. "You know I can't tell you that."

"Yeah, you can. I'm your very own kid!" Arthur said.

"You are." Dad smiled. "And you are excellent at customer service. Also, I love you. But 'confidential' means 'confidential.'"

CHAPTER THIRTY

A rthur told Watson about the missing Red File that night at bedtime, how he was afraid maybe Juan had stolen it, how he was afraid he, Arthur, was a bad person for suspecting Juan had stolen it, how his dad wouldn't give him any info.

As Arthur talked, he felt better. Watson was bossy. Some of her advice had issues. But he liked having her around to talk to, especially when his brain felt overwhelmed.

"I don't see how I'm supposed to solve the mystery," he concluded, "if my own dad won't even answer my questions."

"Do you think there could be a connection between the two mysteries?" Watson asked.

Arthur said, "What two mysteries?"

"The missing Red File and my teacup!" Watson said. *"Duh."*

Watson wasn't usually sarcastic, and now Arthur felt bad. He could have asked his grandmother about the teacup that morning, and he hadn't. In truth, he had forgotten.

"I don't see how," Arthur said, thinking out loud. "There can't be anything about the teacup in the Red File. It was never in the UUI at all."

"They're both mysteries," Watson pointed out. "Isn't that a connection? And they both have to do with the store."

"I guess," Arthur said doubtfully. "And I'll work on your mystery too, Watson. I promise."

"Hmph." Watson sniffed. "You've said *that* before."

On Sunday afternoon Ramona helped Dad paint a banner to welcome Jennifer Y back from her race. They didn't know if she'd won or anything, only that she had finished before ten that same morning, after starting around dawn on Saturday. Finishing before noon meant she had run the whole hundred miles and earned a medal that said so. She was supposed to be back at work on Monday.

Arthur thought he'd get to help with the banner too, but instead Randolph presented him with three big boxes of shoes to enter into the UUI. Arthur would be doing this on his own because Veda had left a message that she wasn't coming in. Her excuse was swim practice, but Arthur knew that the real reason was what Grandpa had said to Juan.

The shoes in the boxes had all come from estates, which made them the shoes of dead people, which for some reason, everyone agreed, were creepier than the clothes of dead people. Arthur's job was to spray each pair with Lysol to get rid of stinky-foot smell, then categorize them by type (athletic, casual, formal, sandal, slipper) and size.

Sorting shoes was always a terrible job, and without Veda it was even more terrible, which is why, after dinner that night, Arthur did something amazing: he phoned Veda for the second time in two days.

He couldn't say "I missed you" because that would be weird. Instead he said, "I don't see why if Juan and your mom still cleaned my grandparents' house yesterday—after, you know, what my grandpa said—then you couldn't have worked at the store today like usual too."

Veda said, "Hi, Arthur. I explained already. Swim practice."

Arthur was lying on his back on the floor, his feet up

on his bed, the blood-to-brain position he hoped would make him smarter. If he was going to be a good detective, he obviously needed extra blood-to-brain.

"Well, are you gonna have longer swim practice next Sunday, too?" he asked.

"I don't know yet," she said.

Arthur sighed. When you thought about it, having friends was a pain. Family you were stuck with—and mouse ghosts that were haunting you—but friends were optional. Arthur thought he could see why people played video games and watched TV and gave up on live humans. Maybe he should do the same thing.

On the other hand, he was used to having Veda around. She was familiar, like the tasks at the store. Also, let's say you had to sort the shoes of dead people? In that case friends could be helpful.

"I am sorry about my grandpa being insulting," Arthur said.

"He is pretty terrible," Veda said.

"He likes you, though," Arthur pointed out.

"Yeah," Veda said, "and how does *that* work? I'm just as Mexican—as Latinx, I guess—as Juan is."

"It might be because he knows you." Arthur had

thought about this. "He thinks of you as *you*, not part of, I don't know—a group? But he doesn't know Juan. Grandma tried to talk to him. He says he didn't do anything wrong. He says he doesn't see what the big deal is."

"*You* should talk to him," Veda said.

"I'm talking to you," Arthur said. "I'm apologizing."

Veda didn't say anything.

"Uh . . . can I ask another question?" Arthur said. "Remember how once you said you didn't trust Juan? Tattoos and everything?"

"That's not the same thing," Veda said.

"I don't mean that it's the same thing," Arthur said. "But you remember, right? So what I want to know is, do you like Juan better now? Do you trust him?"

"My mom does," Veda said.

Arthur had seen enough movies to know that when grown-ups *liked* people—icky romance and all that—they were not always smart, or not as smart as Veda. "What about you?"

It was quiet again before Veda said, "Yeah. I do now. Juan is funny. Also, he's good to my mom. That counts more than tattoos."

CHAPTER THIRTY-ONE

At the store the next afternoon Arthur learned something that rocked his universe, or at least the part occupied by his family.

First thing when he got there, though, he saw Jennifer Y and gave her props on the ultra race.

"I can't believe you even came in to work," he said. "You ran a hundred miles this weekend!"

They were standing on the customer side of the cash counter, Jennifer leaning against it. "Yeah." She smiled. "I know."

Arthur could see she was moving slowly, that the back of her neck was sunburned, that both knees had multiple Band-Aids.

More striking was her face. No Band-Aids there, just a big smile that wouldn't quit.

Arthur thought of Watson. "Do you feel a *glowing sense of accomplishment*?" he asked.

Jennifer laughed. "I hadn't thought of those words exactly, but yeah, I'd say so."

"Would you ever do such a crazy thing again?" Arthur asked.

"Totally," she said. "In fact, I'm making plans for next year. Hey, Officer Bernstein! Good to see you."

Officer Bernstein approached from the direction of Housewares. He had a shopping basket over his arm, and in it the same red pepper mill he'd been looking at a couple of Sundays before.

"Congratulations, Jennifer," he said, and very nearly smiled. Jennifer thanked him.

Arthur asked if he was planning to buy, finally, the pepper mill.

"European-made," said Officer Bernstein. "Do I still get the discount?"

"That can be arranged," Arthur said. "And perhaps you'd like a grinder for sea salt to go with it? Or cruets for oil and vinegar? Or—"

Officer Bernstein held up his hand. "Just the pepper mill, Arthur."

"Excellent choice," Arthur said. "I'll be happy to ring you up."

Jennifer did not do a ton of work that afternoon. First she and Officer Bernstein assessed her splits, which means how fast she had run different sections of the race, and then they talked elevation changes, and the times of other runners around her age.

Arthur had never known there was so much math involved in plain old running; the idea did not make it more tempting.

Later, other customers asked Jen about the banner over the door, which read: CONGRATS, JEN, OUR ULTRA CLERK! And some of them wanted to hear about the race. "The first mile . . . ," Arthur heard Jennifer say as he helped a customer pick out a set of pot holders, and later, "Then there was mile twenty-seven. That's when . . ."

She didn't seem to mind repeating the story.

Monday was Randolph's day off, so Arthur was surprised to see him sorting colored markers in Art Supplies.

"What are you doing here?" Arthur asked.

"Killing time, uh-*huh*," Randolph said. "I'm s'posed to take your grandpa to a doctor's appointment, but he says he's not ready to go."

"Why—" Arthur started to ask, but Randolph was way ahead of him.

"Your grandma's getting ready for company tonight,

cooking, I think. So he asked me to be the chauffeur."

"Got it," Arthur said. "Is Grandpa okay?"

"He says he is. Your mom isn't so sure. He's been poorly lately. You know. Anyway, if I can help him out, I'm happy to. He helped me when I needed it."

Arthur was surprised. "He did? My *grandpa*?"

The markers had been in multicolor heaps in a collection of shoeboxes. Now Randolph ordered a fistful of red into one can, a smaller fistful of green into a second. "You want to grab the yellow ones?" he asked Arthur.

Arthur nodded and began sorting. "So, my grandpa?" he said.

"He probably wouldn't want me to tell you this," Randolph said. "I mean, if no one's told you this already."

"I won't say anything," Arthur said, and he might've added "Cross my heart" but remembered the razzing he'd taken over owning a teacup. Were guys allowed to say "cross my heart"? Anyway, he didn't.

"Well, I told you that story about how your good friend Officer Bernstein arrested me that time?" Randolph continued.

Arthur nodded.

"It was your grandpa who bailed me out, helped me find an apartment, too."

"Oh, wow," Arthur said. "I thought . . . That is . . . I didn't think . . ."

Arthur remembered something about his family helping Randolph but had assumed that meant his mom and dad.

"You didn't think your grandpa had a kind heart?" Randolph said.

Arthur started on the purple markers. "I guess that's about right."

"Your grandpa has his moments," Randolph said. "Uh-*huh*. And now I think I'll go remind him of his appointment one more time . . . unless, that is, your friend the policeman is back there with him in the office?"

"I'm pretty sure Officer Bernstein left," Arthur said.

"See you tomorrow, then," Randolph said. "Oh—and I think you missed a couple o' those yellow markers."

For the next few minutes Arthur thought only of sorting markers. Then he stood back to admire the effect, each color in its own shiny can. And then he considered what Randolph had said.

Before now Arthur had figured he knew his grandpa well. Grandpa was someone who cared about his family and the business he'd started. He was also so crotchety that, if he came to dinner, you had to be careful what you said, so crotchety that sometimes Grandma had to take a break and run away.

But now Arthur had learned something new, something that didn't fit. Grandpa cared about other people, unlucky people like Randolph used to be. And Grandpa could be generous.

People, his grandpa at least, were more complicated than Arthur had ever expected, which meant the universe was more complicated too, which meant—well, what exactly?

Arthur thought he would have to spend a lot more time with his legs in the air, letting blood into his brain, if he was going to figure the universe out.

A customer looking for a "comfortable chair, preferably a neutral color, clean but inexpensive" interrupted Arthur's thoughts. That customer was followed by another who wanted a "good, old-fashioned toaster" and a third who needed "any old ski jacket, provided it's warm and sort of fits." Arthur helped them all, for a fact, solved their problems. That was the thing about customer service. In the universe of Universal Trash, the problems were uncomplicated.

At a little after five, Arthur's boss, aka Dad, sent him home. Upstairs he found his mom in the living room reading.

"You're home from work early," he said when she looked up. "Oh gosh, are you okay?"

Mom's eyes were red, her cheeks streaked with tears. "It's just the book," she said, sniffling. "I came home to finish it before book group." She held it up. *Of Mice and Men.*

"I don't get it," Arthur said. "Why read a book that makes you cry?"

Mom shrugged. "Because it's great literature?" she said. "Because it sort of helps when sad things happen to you? And because it's beautiful, I guess."

"Sadness is beautiful?" Arthur asked.

Mom shrugged and looked down at the book. "I've only got a couple more pages, Arthur."

Arthur said, "Okay. I get it. I'll let you read."

In a puzzling universe one thing was for sure. Arthur never wanted to read a book that made him cry that hard.

CHAPTER THIRTY-TWO

t was because of the Prairie Dog Stomp that Grandma noticed her pearl necklace was gone.

Grandma wasn't even planning to wear her necklace to the Stomp; Mom was. And that Tuesday, Mom phoned Grandma and asked to borrow it to go with her green dress. Grandma said of course, and she looked in her jewelry box, then her backup jewelry box, and then some random other boxes kept in random other drawers.

She could not find the pearl necklace.

So Grandma phoned Mom back and said it was the strangest thing, but the pearls seemed to be missing.

It wasn't till Wednesday dinner that Arthur found all this out. The dinner that night was Arthur's least favorite, a vegetable omelet, which was something his dad put together in a hurry when there were sad, limp vegetables to use up. In Arthur's opinion the only way a vegetable omelet was edible was if it was covered with sour cream and salsa, and they were out of sour cream.

"What do the pearls look like?" Ramona asked her mother. "Have I seen them before? Arthur's taking all the salsa."

"It's a double strand with an emerald clasp," Mom said. "I thought of them because the clasp is the same color as my dress. Grandma never wears them. They just sit around in her jewelry box. Arthur? Leave some salsa for the rest of us, okay?"

Arthur paused in his spooning and looked at his mom. "Huh. That's funny."

"Would you please for gosh sake pass the salsa?" Ramona asked.

Dad looked over. "What's funny?"

Arthur passed the salsa. "Only because lately I've heard about a zillion customers say stuff sits around in a jewelry box, like that guy Mr. Worth, the one who looks like a professor, and he bought that watch . . . ?" Arthur paused midbite and stared straight ahead. *"Huh."*

"Huh?" his dad repeated.

When Arthur didn't react, his mom looked up. *"Huh?"*

"Arthur's in space," Ramona said.

Arthur snapped out of it.

"I am not," he told Ramona. "It's just I remembered Mr. Worth asked who brought the watch in, and I couldn't tell him because it was in the Red File. And now the Red File is gone."

Dad nodded. "Coincidence, I'd say. But I do remember the watch. It had an unusual monogram on it. *ABC* or something."

"*XYZ,*" Arthur said. "What did Mr. Worth bring in this time, Dad? Did Grandma take it?"

Dad nodded. "An amethyst brooch. Not exactly in style, but attractive to the right buyer."

Mom said, "Is the Red File still missing?"

Dad was chewing, and he nodded.

"Were there a lot of cards in it?" she asked.

Dad swallowed. "About twenty-five active ones, but I keep the archive in the same box. There might be two hundred of those, maybe more. They don't matter much because the merchandise has already sold. We got our money. But if the police ever had a question . . ." He shrugged. "It almost never happens. We know most of our consigners. And maybe it helps that Officer Bernstein likes to hang out at the store. Keeps bad guys away."

"So what will you do about the missing file? Assuming it doesn't turn up," Mom said.

"Try to remember what's in it, then make new cards," Dad said.

"So it doesn't really matter that the Red File is gone?" Arthur said, which was another way to say, "I spent all that time searching and thinking for nothing?"

"What matters is that it disappeared," Dad said. "Why would someone take it? Or maybe worse—did I set it somewhere and forget? In which case, I am losing it."

It was quiet for a couple of minutes, nothing but chewing and bodies shifting in chairs. Finally Dad looked around and said, "It would be nice if someone reassured me that I'm *not* losing it."

"You still make a decent omelet," Mom said. "Is there any more salsa, Ramona?"

Ramona passed the salsa.

"So I thought of a motive for stealing the Red File," Arthur said, "but if you can just make a new one, it might not make sense."

"Go ahead, Detective," Dad said. "Tell us."

"Maybe whoever stole it was someone whose name was in there, someone trying to be extra super sure their name never got out, someone who had stolen whatever it was they'd brought in to consign."

Arthur's dad nodded. "Right. I thought of that too."

"But now," Arthur went on, "it looks like, if somebody really didn't want their name known, they'd have to eliminate you too, Dad."

"Arthur!" Mom said.

"Sounds like something from an old movie," Dad said.

"I'm being logical," Arthur said. "Isn't logical good? In school they say it is."

"I like logical," Mom said. "I don't like being scared to death."

"If it's any help," Dad said, "consider this. The most expensive item in the store is priced at around five thousand dollars. And the penalty for, uh . . . *eliminating* a person, a person such as me, is life in prison. So for half of five thousand dollars—the consigner's cut of the sale? Not worth the risk. Now, if we had some massive diamond or something . . . but we don't."

Ramona stood up. "I'm done with dinner."

"I see that, Ramona," Mom said. "Would you like to clear the table while you're up?"

"Not especially," Ramona said.

"Ramona?" Dad frowned.

"I didn't say I *wouldn't*." Ramona picked up her own plate.

"Thank you for clearing the table, Ramona," Mom said.

Ramona put her plate on the counter, returned to the table, collected her mother's plate and then her father's. "I can be logical too," she said, "if you care."

"We care," Dad said. "What are you thinking, Mo?"

"I am thinking," Ramona said, "that the Red File and Grandma's pearls disappeared around the same time—so it's *logical* that the same person swiped both."

CHAPTER THIRTY-THREE

At bedtime Arthur and Watson agreed that Ramona's logic wasn't logical.

"Lots of things happen at the same time that have nothing to do with each other," Watson said. "Right at this moment, for example, I'm balanced on your bedpost swishing my tail while Officer Bernstein is arresting a bad guy and Veda is herding the niños. But that doesn't make those things related."

Arthur sat up against his pillows. "Wait a sec. How do you know what Officer Bernstein and Veda are doing?" He was hoping Watson's supernatural powers were improving.

"Those were just examples," Watson said. "In Kenya some lion is probably eating some zebra, while out in the ocean on some cruise ship, a handsome young man is about to propose to a beautiful young woman. And those things aren't related. Or maybe in the Wild West, a cowboy is about to lasso a bull, while in Rome a chef is about to pull a perfect pizza from the oven. But those things—"

"I get the idea, Watson," Arthur said. He was kind of wondering how Watson knew about cruise ships and Kenya and cowboys. Supernatural powers? But he didn't ask. Watson seemed to be in a chatty mood, and he, Arthur, was sleepy.

"I don't suppose anyone has brought in your grand-mother's pearls for the store to sell?" Watson asked.

Arthur lay back down. "I don't think the thief would be that dumb," he said. "Either Dad or Grandpa might recognize those pearls. And Grandma's there too, some-times. Anyway, for a fact, we don't know that the pearls and the Red File disappeared at the same time. Grandma's pearls might've been gone for a while. She only noticed now because Mom asked for them."

"Yes, yes, I see," said Watson. "And whether the mys-teries are related or not, you have your work cut out for you. One teacup found and two things missing—the Red File and the necklace. I think, Detective Popper, that you had better get busy."

Arthur stifled a sigh. Watson was ordering him around again. But maybe it wasn't a bad thing? Sometimes Arthur wasn't sure what to do with himself, and now he had someone to tell him. True, Watson was only a dead rodent. But she was full of ideas.

"I wish the mysteries seemed more important," Arthur said. "The teacup is chipped. Dad can re-create the Red File from memory. Grandma hardly ever wore those pearls."

"Do you wish someone were dead? Someone besides me, that is. Then you could solve a murder mystery," Watson said.

Arthur thought of his dad, the talk about "eliminating" him because he knew what was in the Red File. "No, definitely not," he said. "Good night, Watson."

"Good night, Arthur. Sweet dreams."

Arthur's grandmother had read him stories where dreams predicted the future. Arthur's own dreams, as best he could remember, were mostly a useless jumble.

But that night must have been different.

The next morning when he woke up, he was thinking of the pearl necklace and that phrase he'd heard so much: "just sitting around in the jewelry box."

When he sat up and rubbed his eyes, he saw the teacup across the room on its shelf, and a phrase popped into his head: the perfect crime.

Like "rigor mortis," this was probably something he'd heard in a movie on TV.

Rigor mortis is the way a body stiffens up after it dies.

The "perfect crime," Arthur thought as he pulled on shorts, sniffed his T-shirt, and tugged it over his head, was one you could commit knowing for sure you'd never get blamed.

And why would that be?

Maybe because no one knew it had happened, no one knew that there'd even been a crime at all.

Okay, Arthur thought, *but why did my dreams put that into my head?*

Arthur went into the kitchen, smiled at his mom, poured himself a bowl of Frosted Flakes (A treat! On sale two-for-one at Ideal Market!), poured milk into the bowl, sat down, and ate.

He was slurping the last of the very sweet milk when an answer came.

"Mom!" he said, and his voice was so sharp that she startled and sloshed the coffee she'd been sipping.

"Oh my goodness, Arthur, you scared me," she said. "Is everything okay?"

Arthur blinked. He couldn't believe it. Maybe all that

blood-to-brain had worked? "I think I figured it out!" he said.

Mom nodded, rose from her chair, tore off a paper towel. "That's great, honey. I'm glad. Something to do with school? Math homework?" She dampened the towel with tap water, then dabbed at the spot of coffee. "Do I need to change my blouse, do you think?"

Ramona came in. "Are there more Frosted Flakes, or did Arthur eat them all?"

"There's another whole box, Ramona," Mom said.

Ramona glanced up. "I can't reach it," she announced.

Still fussing with her blouse, Mom said, "Arthur, would you get the cereal down for Ramona, please?"

Arthur got up from the table and pulled the Frosted Flakes from the shelf. Apparently, Mom did not care that he had figured it out. Aloud he said, "Maybe Officer Bernstein will care."

Ramona was in a good mood. "Sure," she said. "I mean, everyone likes Frosted Flakes."

"I think my blouse will do," Mom said. "It's not like I have to go to court. Oh, and good for you on your homework, Arthur. High five?"

Arthur had no idea what his mom was talking about, but he high-fived her anyway.

"Remember Edie is coming over after school, Mom. Are you coming home early, or will Dad be here?" Ramona said.

"Oh, shoot, that's right," Mom said. "Someone will be here, Ramona. Some responsible grown-up, I mean. I just don't know who."

Arthur, meanwhile, was making plans. *I've got to take a look in the jewelry case at the store,* he thought, *and talk to Grandma, and ride down to Pearl Street on my bike. Maybe Veda will come with me.*

Later I'll explain to Mom. I'll explain to everybody.

Probably I'll get some kind of reward!

For once he felt good about himself, not quite the glowing sense of accomplishment Jennifer Y felt, but better than usual. *Maybe I'm good at something besides customer service after all.*

"See ya tonight, Mom. Bye, Mo," he said.

Ramona looked up. "'Mo'?"

But Arthur was out the door, grabbing his backpack, and hurrying down the stairs.

CHAPTER THIRTY-FOUR

That day during library time Arthur tried to return *The Legend of King Arthur.*

"How did you like it?" Mrs. Danneberg asked. "The plot's tricky, didn't you think?"

"It is," Arthur said.

"I especially like the part where Arthur meets the man in the moon," Mrs. Danneberg said.

"That part was good," Arthur agreed.

"Arthur." Mrs. Danneberg leveled a stare. "I made that up. It's not in the story. You didn't read it, did you?"

Arthur was embarrassed. "I . . . couldn't get into it," he said. He had heard his mom say this before about books; he thought it sounded good.

"Did you *try*, Arthur?" Mrs. Danneberg asked.

"I did!" Arthur said, but his cheeks were hot, which probably meant he was blushing.

Mrs. Danneberg raised her eyebrows over the stare.

"I mean, I opened it," he said, "and so forth."

"How about if you try it for another week, Arthur?" Mrs. Danneberg pushed the book back. "And promise me you'll read at least the first chapter. If after that you still 'can't get into it,' I will understand."

Arthur liked Mrs. Danneberg, even if she was an eye roller. He did not want to disappoint her. "Okay, Mrs. Danneberg. I will."

The bell rang, and Arthur waited for Veda outside the library. He hadn't seen her before school, and he had a lot to explain. As soon as she caught up, he started in.

Veda listened a little, then scrunched her eyes and shook her head. "Wait, wait, wait, Arthur. Slow down! Who committed the perfect crime? I don't understand."

Arthur paused in his explanation. "We-e-ell . . . ," he said. "I guess I don't know *who* exactly. Not yet anyway. But someone did. And then they stole the Red File to, like, to cover it up, cover their tracks. You know what the Red File is, right?"

"Of course I do," Veda said. "And you told me it got lost. But who would steal it?"

Apparently detectives not only needed to be smart; they also needed to be patient. "Veda," Arthur said in the calm voice of a preschool teacher, "that is pre-cise-ly what I am trying to ex-plain."

Meanwhile, around them, kids streamed by on their way to class, and above them the hall clock's second hand kept circling. Ninety seconds till the bell rang, eighty-five seconds, eighty . . . The crowd in the hallway was thinning out. Already they would have to hurry or be late to class.

"Look—there's no time right now," Arthur said. "Can you come over on Saturday? We can ride our bikes downtown."

"I don't know, Arthur. Maybe," Veda said.

"Are you still mad at my family?" Arthur asked.

"Maybe." Veda glanced up. "Bell's gonna ring—see you!" And she took off running.

The bell's echo had faded by the time Arthur ducked through the door to his classroom, but Mr. Racker was facing the whiteboard and never noticed he was late. *Maybe this is a good sign*, Arthur thought, and he was optimistic for the rest of the morning. At lunchtime, he even thought of telling the guys what he'd tried to tell Veda. Since he'd been razzed about the teacup, he worried that his status with them was shaky. Maybe if he told them he was solving a mystery, they would be impressed?

But by the time he sat down at the usual table, he'd decided against it. Wouldn't Zeke give him grief about *jewelry* the way he had about the teacup? And besides, the whole thing was complicated. He hadn't been able to get even Veda to understand, and Veda already knew how the store worked, knew about the Red File too.

The explanation can wait, Arthur thought. *Maybe till they see me on the TV news!*

Arthur stopped by the store after school. He wasn't scheduled to work, but he had detecting to do.

In Electronics, Jennifer Y was helping someone sort through power cords. She was still moving like her knees were stiff, Arthur noticed.

"Hey, Arthur." She grinned, then turned back to her customer. "It really depends on the connector," she said. "It's for a tablet, right?"

Arthur made his way through Office Supplies and Holiday till he got to the jewelry case by the counter. The gold pendant earrings were still there. Arthur tried hard to remember the woman who had pointed them out to him, said they looked like the ones her mother gave her, but he had helped a lot of customers since then. She had bought a bowl, he thought. For a wedding present? Oh, and hadn't she said she'd never been in the store before?

The other customer's name, Molly Hart, he remembered because she'd been in only last week. Now he found the bracelet she had pointed out. Her aunt had given it to her? Something like that. Anyway, it, too, "just sat around in the jewelry box."

Hadn't Molly Hart been a new customer as well?

"I didn't know you were into vintage jewelry, Arthur. Are you looking for something in particular?" Randolph was behind the cash counter, finishing up a receipt.

"Not at the present time," Arthur said. "But may I see that bracelet?" He pointed. "Oh, and those earrings, too?"

Randolph fussed in the drawer, found the key, opened the case. "These?" He handed the items to Arthur. "You have excellent taste, sir. Shall I wrap them up, or would you like to wear them home?"

Arthur looked at the tag on the earring box. "My ears aren't pierced, in case you didn't know."

Randolph picked up a sharp pencil and aimed it in the general direction of Arthur's earlobes. "I can take care of that, sir," he said.

Arthur said, "*Ouch.* No thanks."

Randolph took the box back and looked at the tag on the box himself. "The consigner's name is in the Red File," he said, "the one that's missing. Why are you so interested?"

Arthur should've been ready for this question, but he wasn't, and all he could think to say was, "Idle curiosity?" He had heard that in a movie too.

Randolph cocked his head skeptically.

"You don't know who brought these in, do you?" Arthur asked.

"Me?" Randolph shook his head. "Your dad handles most of the consignments. You know that. Besides, everything in the Red File is—"

"Confidential. I know." Arthur was tempted to explain what he had figured out: someone, some thief, was committing the perfect crime, stealing jewelry that people hardly knew they owned—jewelry just sitting around in a jewelry box—bringing it to the store to sell, and then collecting the money when it did.

There were a few details Arthur didn't know, like how many pieces of jewelry the thief had brought in, or how many had sold, or how much all the jewelry was worth.

Then there was the identity of the thief. He didn't know that, either.

Arthur remembered the pocket watch Mr. Worth had bought, the one with *XYZ*. That record had been in the Red File too.

"Do you mind if I take a look at the Current UUI box for jewelry?" Arthur asked Randolph.

Randolph stepped forward so Arthur could get at the shelves behind him. "Have at it," he said and then, to a woman walking toward the cash counter, "May I help you, ma'am? Those badger figurines are sweet. Perhaps you'd be interested in a cabinet to display them?"

Arthur slipped behind Randolph, took the box from its shelf, and flipped through the few cards categorized Jewelry, subcategory Fine Jewelry. These cards represented every item in the locked jewelry case—all the store's fine (not costume) jewelry. This was the one for the earrings:

011823DJ

S, J, F, E, g

Red

$250

Arthur translated almost without thinking: The earrings had come in on January 18 of this year. His dad had checked them in—*D* for "Dan" in the first line. The next line meant small [S], jewelry [J], fine [F], earrings [E], and gold [g]. The consigner was "Red," meaning the name was in the Red File—confidential. And the value was $250.

Next Arthur found the card for the bracelet and looked it over.

111622DJ

S, J, F, Bt, g

Red

$375

There was nothing unusual about either card except that the consigner was in the missing Red File. Oh, and each had come in around the same time of the month. Was that important?

Arthur didn't know, but just in case he grabbed a piece of paper from the drawer under the cash counter and noted down the dates.

Then he looked for the watch under subcategory Timepieces, but, as he'd expected, it wasn't there. Since it had already sold, Laura, the bookkeeper, would have moved the record from the Current UUI box by the register to the Annual UUI in the boxes in the office.

Arthur put the box back, told Randolph, "See ya later," and walked to the office. Inside were his dad and Officer Bernstein, each sitting behind a desk, each looking unusually serious, his dad frowning, Officer Bernstein even sadder than usual.

"Hey, kiddo," Dad said after a second. "Do you need something? You've got the afternoon off, you know."

"Hello, Arthur," Officer Bernstein said.

Arthur smiled at Officer Bernstein, said, "Just checking on something," went to the shelf that held the Annual files, and pulled down the box labeled JEWELRY.

"What are you looking for?" Dad asked.

Arthur was annoyed with his dad for not telling him whether Juan had brought in items to consign, whether Juan's name was in the Red File, in other words. But *fine.* If Dad wouldn't reveal confidential information to his own *child*, then that same child, Arthur, would go ahead and solve the mystery himself.

"Well, Dad," he said now, "for a fact, it's confidential."

CHAPTER THIRTY-FIVE

Dad didn't say anything to that. In fact, neither he nor Officer Bernstein said a word as Arthur riffled through the cards in the box, found subcategory Fine Jewelry, then Timepieces, then Pocket Watches, and finally the card he wanted:

021523DJ

S, J, F, PW, g (Special Note: Tiffany, Engraving XYZ)

Red

$895

In other words it had come in on February 15, been accepted by Dan—aka Dad. It was a PW—pocket watch—the consigner information was in the Red File, and the price was $895.

The date, Arthur noted, was also in the middle of the month, and he wrote it down. Maybe it was hanging out with Officer Bernstein that made Arthur notice numbers. Whatever it was, he decided to look at a calendar to see whether those three dates—11/16/22, 1/18/23, and 2/15/23—had anything else in common.

Arthur put the card back into the box and the box back into its place. Only then did he realize that the office was strangely quiet, and he looked from his dad to sad-faced Officer Bernstein. "Is everything okay?" he asked.

"Well," Dad said, "your grandpa—" He glanced at Officer Bernstein.

"What about Grandpa?" Arthur said, and he felt his knees get weak. He was mad at his grandpa, but still . . .

"Oh, no, sorry," Dad said quickly. "Grandpa's okay. Physically okay. But he's got this idea—" Dad shook his head.

"What idea?" Arthur asked.

Dad explained. It turned out Arthur wasn't the only one who had thought over the puzzle of the missing Red File and the missing pearl necklace. Grandpa had too. But his conclusion was different from Arthur's.

Grandpa was convinced Juan had stolen both.

In fact, Grandpa was so sure Juan was a thief that he had phoned the Boulder PD.

"An officer is interviewing Juan right now," Dad said.

"But Juan didn't do anything!" Arthur said.

Dad shook his head. "I hope not. But why do you say that?"

"Because of Veda," Arthur said. "She wasn't sure she liked Juan at first, but now she is. She says he's a good guy. Also, like you said before, Maria is super careful who she hires."

Dad nodded. "I hear you, kiddo. But I'm not sure any of that will hold up in a court of law."

"So what does Grandpa say?" Arthur asked. "Is it just his, uh . . . prejudice? Like what he said in the store last week?"

"Grandpa's evidence is what they call circumstantial," Dad said. "Juan was in their house cleaning with Maria on Saturday. Grandma missed the pearl necklace on Tuesday, so it's possible that Saturday is when it disappeared. And Juan was here in the office last week too—possibly the day the Red File disappeared. According to your grandpa, Juan is the only person in the world who was in the right place at the right time to steal both."

Arthur thought for a moment. "But couldn't some thief have broken into Grandma and Grandpa's house?"

Dad looked at Officer Bernstein, and Officer Bernstein answered. "Unlikely. A burglar wouldn't have gone to the trouble to break in and take only one necklace. I still think the most likely explanation is that the necklace is lost. But if this is a crime at all, it seems like one of opportunity. That is, someone who happened to be in the house anyway noticed the necklace, or an open jewelry box or whatever, and the someone took advantage."

Arthur's own theory fit the crime-of-opportunity idea, and it looked bad for Juan. Still, he didn't believe that Veda was wrong. "Someone else might have been in their house and taken it," Arthur said. "Isn't that possible?"

"Sure," Dad said, "but, honestly, Grandma and Grandpa don't have that many visitors anymore, not even us."

Arthur hadn't thought about this till now, but he saw that it was true. When he was little, he and his family used to go to his grandparents' house for dinner pretty often. Lately, though, when they saw Grandma and Grandpa, it was either here at the store or in their own apartment upstairs, or sometimes at a restaurant. But then Arthur thought of something else. "Grandma had company this week. That's why Juan and Maria were cleaning on Saturday."

"Company?" Dad repeated.

Arthur nodded. "Her book group. Remember? We ate dinner early Monday because she had to get there. I even know the book they were reading. It's called *Of Mice and Men*."

Officer Bernstein sighed. "That's a very sad book."

CHAPTER THIRTY-SIX

Mom was a lawyer with a fancy computer in her office near the courthouse, an expensive laptop at home, and the latest phone. Basically, she was the opposite of Grandpa, whose idea of modern technology was file cards in boxes on a shelf.

But Mom was old-fashioned in one way.

She kept her not-work appointments on a paper calendar on the wall of her office at home.

Arthur thought this was great because he never had to worry about a Christmas gift for Mom. Every year he gave her a calendar, and every year she said, "Perfect! I love it!"

Last Christmas, Arthur had picked out a calendar with black-and-white pictures from Colorado history. Now he was by her desk, studying the picture for this month, May, which showed a bunch of white guys with mustaches and hats in a store, or maybe a bar? Arthur had to look twice to notice there was a little donkey in the picture too.

What was a donkey doing there?

The photo was labeled 1893, and Arthur wondered if people in 1893 had had donkeys instead of dogs. That would have been cool, but it didn't seem likely.

Anyway, Mom's calendar was the easiest place to look for a pattern for the dates in the UUI, the dates when the jewelry had come into the store. He wasn't really expecting to find anything, but he wanted to keep detecting. Now it seemed even more important. He had to help Juan.

Having thought about the donkey, Arthur looked at the dates in May. This coming Saturday, May 20, was the Prairie Dog Stomp, seven thirty p.m. at the Dairy Arts Center. The Sunday before Memorial Day, the family had tickets to a Rockies game in Denver. Mom was having lunch with her friends Laura and Sarah next Wednesday. The Wednesday after that, she was taking a walk with her friend Angela.

Pretty boring, Arthur thought—except for baseball.

Looking backward, he saw *Book Group, Mom's house, 7 p.m.* on the previous Monday night, May 15. Book group stood out because the note was written in purple ink. Arthur pulled from his back pocket the paper where he had written the jewelry dates, and paged back through the calendar to see if there was anything special about January 18 and February 15, the dates when the earrings and the watch from the Red File had come in. For now, he couldn't check the date for the bracelet; he didn't have the calendar for November of the year before.

Both January 18 and February 15 were Wednesdays, he noticed right away.

And there was something else, too. They were both Wednesdays two days after his mom's Monday book group.

Was that a coincidence?

Arthur had a brainstorm. Mom's helpful calendar not only noted "Book Group" but also who was hosting. He flipped back to the month of January, looked again at the purple notation: *Book Group, Malarky, 7 p.m.*

Malarky! That was the name of the woman who pointed out the earrings. And two days after book group at her house, Dad had accepted for consignment a pair of earrings just like hers, the ones that had sat around in her jewelry box.

Quickly Arthur looked again at February 13, and when he did, his heart went *thud.* The host that month was someone named Sandy Young. "Young" with a *Y*—the initial on the pocket watch that had come into the store two days later.

Arthur sat down in Mom's desk chair, really, really wishing he had the November calendar.

But he could ask Mom about that later.

For now, his theory looked good. No—his theory looked *brilliant*! Someone was stealing jewelry from the book group hosts and bringing it to Universal Trash to consign. Only, this month, when the someone had stolen Grandma's necklace, they had taken it somewhere else, worried it would be recognized at Universal Trash because of Grandma's connection to the store.

Arthur pulled out his phone and texted Veda: **We can help Juan. Call me.**

Then he waited.

Did Veda have lacrosse on Thursday? he wondered. *Or field hockey? Chess club?* Or she might be busy with the niños.

The other possibility was that she knew Grandpa had called the BPD, and she was mad—*again.*

"Arthur?" a voice called from the living room. "Is that you?"

"Yes, it's me. Hi, Grandma." Arthur didn't know what his grandma was doing there, but it was lucky. He could ask her about the book group in November. Oh—and maybe about the teacup, too. Except now the teacup seemed even less important.

Also, he was hungry.

"Can you meet me in the kitchen?" he called.

CHAPTER THIRTY-SEVEN

Arthur opened the refrigerator, opened the vegetable drawer, took out one baby carrot, and ate it for good health. Then he opened a cupboard and grabbed a box of Cheez-Its and ate two handfuls. He was considering climbing the stepladder to see if there was a box of cookies up high, when Grandma came in. She had a book in her hand.

"I'm just trying to finish this." She held the book up— *Of Mice and Men.* "The girls are in Ramona's room. At least I hope they are. They've been awfully quiet."

What girls? Arthur thought, and then he remembered. "Oh, Edie's here," he said. "I thought you had to finish that by Monday."

Grandma said, "I ran out of time. But the women in my book group liked it, and so I'm carrying on."

"Speaking of your book group, Grandma. Do you have a sec? I have a couple of questions."

"You do?" Grandma laid the book on the kitchen table. "Okay, I guess, but that is just weird, Arthur. No one in world history has ever had a question about his grandmother's book group."

Arthur nodded. "I know, right? I am unique."

"And good at customer service," Grandma said. "So what's your question?"

"Sandy Young in your book group, does she have a relative, probably a dead relative, with the initials *Z* and *X*?"

"You think I know the initials of Sandy Young's dead relatives?" Grandma asked.

"Not necessarily," Arthur said. "But I have an easier question too."

"This is like *Jeopardy!*," Grandma said. "I'll take Easier Questions about My Book Group for fifty, Arthur."

"Who hosted book group in November last year?" Arthur asked.

Grandma shook her head. "That question is not much easier."

"*Jeopardy!* answers are in the form of questions," Arthur reminded her.

"Right. Was that question supposed to be easier?"

"I hoped it was," Arthur said.

"Oh, I know—wait." Grandma pulled out her phone, tapped it a whole bunch of times, frowned, scrolled, frowned harder, tapped it more times.

"Grandma," Arthur said, "it's okay if—"

"Ha!" Grandma smiled. "Got it! My November calendar for last year. Now just hold on. . . ." More tapping and frowning, but at last she smiled again. "Molly Hart hosted last November. That is, 'Was Molly the book group host last November?'"

"What was the date?" Arthur asked.

"I think I should get more points if I answer that," Grandma said.

"Fine—you can have all the points. For a fact, this can be Final Jeopardy, and you can win, okay?"

"Yippee!" Grandma raised her fist. "It was Monday, November 14."

"Yes!" Arthur pumped his fist in the air.

"Yes?" Grandma repeated. "May I ask what this is all about?"

"Sure, but I won't tell you," Arthur said. "Not yet."

Grandma nodded. "Very mysterious, but I'm glad you're detecting—glad if you're glad, I mean. And now, if you don't mind, I'm going to finish my sad book."

Grandma returned to the living room. Arthur looked down at his phone. Still no text from Veda.

Hoping to update Watson, he went back to his room. He didn't see Watson right away, but he did realize something. Unauthorized entry had taken place. The four pillows on his bed had been flat when he'd left that morning and were now plumped up. The coffee mug where he kept his pencils belonged on the windowsill, and now it was on his desk.

Finally, there was a sweet smell, like lip gloss or fruity shampoo.

"Watson?" he said. "Are you here? Did Ramona invade my space?"

Arthur went to check the teacup and got another surprise. The teacup was gone.

CHAPTER THIRTY-EIGHT

The dancing-bear teacup usually rested on the same shelf as Arthur's collection of Sherlock Holmes mysteries. Now Watson appeared there, nosing out from behind the books. "She did indeed," the mouse said, sitting up on her haunches. "Her friend was with her. I guess you can see that they stole my hangout."

"But why?" Arthur said. "What did they say?"

"I'm afraid I don't understand first graders," Watson said. "Perhaps you'd better ask them?"

Arthur left his room and marched down the hall. *"Ramona!"* he yelled, then opened her door without knocking. "What were you doing in my room? And give me back my teacup!"

"I was never in your room," Ramona said. "Was I, Edie?"

Ramona and Edie were sitting on the floor with a treasure's worth of costume jewelry—some of it decking their bodies, some of it piled between them. In spite of

Ramona's words, Arthur got immediate confirmation that they had been in his room. Ramona's room smelled the same as his—strawberry shampoo, he thought.

Edie blinked and said, "Ummm . . ." She couldn't meet Arthur's eye, must not've been as used to lying as Ramona was.

"Well, I wasn't, and Edie wasn't either, and we are being beautiful, and you aren't allowed to come in without knocking," Ramona said. "So go away."

"I know you were in my room, Ramona. What were you doing there?"

Ramona looked at her brother, narrowed her eyes. "*How* do you know?" she asked.

"Ha! You admit it!" Arthur said.

"I do not. I only said 'How did you know?'" Ramona said.

Arthur wondered what it would be like to have a sister who was less exasperating. Or a brother, why couldn't he have a brother?

"I know because . . . because . . . I could smell you, okay?" Arthur said.

"I am not smelly!" Ramona said. "You take that back! *Grand-maaaa!*"

"Go ahead and tell Grandma if you want. I'll tell her you went into my room when you're not allowed."

"Why aren't you allowed, Ramona?" Edie sounded actually interested. She was an only child. *Must be nice,* Arthur thought.

"First, he's not allowed because he is a creepy boy," Ramona said. "And second, he is not allowed because he and I are having a war."

"No, we're not," Arthur said.

"And when you're having a war," Ramona continued, "you invade enemy territory."

"Invade enemy territory?" Arthur repeated. "Where do you even get this stuff, Ramona? Is there a war in *Frozen* or something?"

"*Frozen* is not the only movie I watch," Ramona said. "And besides that, I go to school. And there was the Civil War."

Arthur couldn't help saying, "Like you even know what that was."

"There was, though, and *somebody* invaded *somebody's* territory, just like we invaded your room, and . . . Oops. I mean—"

"Ha!" Arthur said.

Which is when Grandma opened the door. "Everything okay in here?" she asked.

"No!" Ramona said, obviously ready to recite complaints about her brother. But then she saw her grandmother's face. "Are you *crying*? Are you okay?"

Grandma sniffed. "Just my book. I'll get over it."

Ramona seemed to accept that as normal and got back to her complaining. "Arthur came into my room without knocking!"

"Because Ramona went into my room when she's not allowed," Arthur clarified.

"Liar," Ramona said.

"Ramona," Grandma said.

"Take it back," Arthur said.

"I think your mom's home," Grandma said. "At least, I hear someone on the stairs. Shall we let her adjudicate this? She went to law school."

"Mo-o-o-om!" Ramona yelled.

"You called?" Mom appeared in the doorway. "What's the trouble?"

"She stole my teacup," Arthur said.

"For a *fact,* it's Edie's, and she said I can keep it," Ramona said. "It's just the right size for Bluebell."

"So you admit you were in my room!" Arthur said.

"Who's Bluebell?" Grandma asked.

"She's a cow," Mom said. "Right, Ramona? I got it right this time?"

"And it isn't Edie's teacup, Ramona," Arthur went on. "I mean . . . what do you mean?"

But Ramona didn't have a chance to answer because Mrs. Merdle appeared. "Hello, girls. Hi, Arthur. Ready to go, Edie? Have you had a nice time? Thank Ramona, won't you?" Mrs. Merdle was wearing running clothes again, silver Nikes, black tights, and a blue race T-shirt that read *Colder Boulder*.

Edie ducked her head to remove the necklaces, then stood up, shedding bracelets and earrings as she did. "Thank you, Ramona," she said. "But maybe you should give Arthur back the—"

"No!" Ramona interrupted.

"I didn't realize you owned a cow, Ramona," Grandma said.

"Well, I do, and her barn is in my jammie drawer," Ramona said.

"I'm sure she's very comfortable," Grandma said. "And I must be getting home. Are you coming, Amy?"

She looked at Mrs. Merdle, then at Mom. "Apologies for leaving you with a war on your hands. Perhaps you can arrange a truce."

"A war?" Mom looked from Arthur to Ramona.

"She—" Arthur began.

"No, *he*—" Ramona insisted.

Mom held up her hand. "All right, you two. Work it out yourselves, please. It's my turn to get dinner."

Mom, Grandma, Edie, and Mrs. Merdle all headed for the kitchen, Mom to heat up chili, everyone else to leave for home. As for Arthur, he wanted to yell and stomp and open drawers in search of Watson's teacup, but that would just get him in trouble.

Meanwhile, it was pretty awkward standing there with Ramona glaring at him.

So, with a final scowl, he retreated.

"And stay out!" Ramona called, slamming her door after him—a mistake because it made Arthur even madder.

I will find that teacup! he thought. *And I will get it back! But I will have to be sneaky.*

CHAPTER THIRTY-NINE

That night at bedtime Arthur told Watson what had happened with the teacup, why it wasn't back yet. "But now it's in Ramona's room," Arthur said. "She more or less admitted that. I just have to find it."

Without her hangout, Watson was lounging on top of a Sherlock Holmes book, *A Study in Scarlet*. "What a puzzle," she said. "How could my teacup have belonged to Edie?"

Arthur lay on his bed, facing the opposite wall. His knees were up, his ankles on the headboard. It was the blood-to-brain position.

"I don't know," he said to the ceiling. "Maybe just another Ramona lie, but everything got crazy all of a sudden, so I never asked more, and anyway Ramona wouldn't have answered. At dinner she wouldn't even pass the milk."

"Sibling rivalry is the worst," said Watson. "And did she get in trouble?"

"Hardly at all," Arthur said. "My parents totally spoil her. I wish for once they'd spoil me."

"Perhaps you should talk to Edie," Watson said.

"Talk to a first grader?" Arthur said.

"She's a witness, and you're a detective," Watson said. "It's part of the job."

Arthur didn't want to talk to Edie, but he didn't want to say that either. Instead he told Watson what he'd learned from Grandma, that the jewelry seemed to be stolen from people when they hosted book group.

"So the thief is someone in the book group," Watson said.

"Or someone connected somehow," Arthur said. "But it can't be Susana Malarky, and it can't be Molly Hart, either. Because their stuff was stolen."

"By that logic, it's not your grandmother," Watson said.

"Well, of course not," Arthur said—a little annoyed.

"It could be your mother, though," Watson continued.

"Watson!" Arthur pulled down his legs and spun around on his back. "My mother's not a thief."

Watson's tail swished furiously, and she sat forward. "A detective can't let emotional relationships interfere, you know. A detective considers all options."

"Not that one," Arthur said.

"If your mother did it," Watson said, ignoring Arthur's words, "that would explain why your father won't tell you the names in the Red File. It's to protect her."

Arthur closed his eyes. "No, Watson. Just no."

"All the same, I think you should ask her," Watson said. "And about the teacup, talk to Edie. That teacup may not matter to you, Arthur. But it does matter to *me*. Besides, it's darned uncomfortable on this shelf without it."

Kids at Arthur's school couldn't check their phones in class, which is why Arthur didn't get his grandma's text till Friday lunchtime: **Sand yong gpa Xaviey Zacry. Dose help u?**

Translating Grandma's texts was a little like decoding Grandpa's UUI entries. This one meant: "Sandy Young's grandpa was named Xavier Zachary. Does that help you?"

Yes! Arthur texted back; then he added a whole bunch of hearts and roses.

So now he knew, or thought he knew, that the pocket watch Mr. Worth had bought had probably belonged to Sandy Young's grandfather, because his initials—*X* and *Z* for the first and middle names, *Y* for "Young"—were engraved on it. And *that* meant, probably, it had been stolen from Sandy Young's house when she'd hosted the book group in February, just like Molly Hart's bracelet had been stolen in November, Susana Malarky's earrings in January, and Grandma's necklace at book group on Monday night.

The case was coming together. Even better, the thief couldn't be Juan. Juan wasn't in book group. It was only coincidence that he'd helped clean Grandma's house on Saturday.

Arthur felt good, for once. He imagined solving the case, the glowing sense of accomplishment, telling Veda, bragging to the guys at lunch.

"Hey, Arthur." On her way to sit with her usual peeps, Veda interrupted these thoughts. "I'm sorry I didn't call you back about Juan, but—"

"Don't worry about it, Darth," said Arthur, "but listen. Can you come with me somewhere tomorrow afternoon? It's important. I've been detecting."

Veda looked confused. "Your grandmother's necklace?"

Arthur nodded. "It'll all make sense tomorrow. I promise."

Veda looked skeptical. "I can meet you at the store after lunch, I guess. Text me in the morning."

"Bring your bike," Arthur said.

CHAPTER FORTY

Arthur wasn't on the store's schedule after school that day, but he stopped by the office on his way upstairs. Maybe he could talk to Grandpa B the way Veda wanted him to. Arthur didn't like confrontation. But maybe he could find the courage.

As it turned out, though, Grandpa wasn't there. Instead Arthur found Dad, behind his desk, and Mrs. Merdle. She had made herself comfortable, and Arthur could tell right away that Dad wished she would let him get back to work.

Dad had to be polite, though. She was a good customer.

"Amy came by to return one of Ramona's earrings," Dad explained. "It seems Edie wore it home yesterday by mistake."

"Clipped in her hair like a barrette," Mrs. Merdle said. "I told her I was bringing it right back today. I wouldn't want anyone to think my granddaughter was a thief."

"Innocent mistake," Dad said. "I'll be sure Ramona gets it, not that she'll even notice. She has a ton of junk jewelry in that box of hers."

"It's been very nice to see you, Mrs. Merdle," Arthur said. "I'm going upstairs to get a snack and—"

"Hey, Arthur," Dad said as if he'd just had a great idea. "How about if you show Amy, Mrs. Merdle, I mean, that walnut table we've got out front? Didn't you say you might need something for your new dining room, Amy?"

Arthur did not want to show Mrs. Merdle the walnut table. He wanted a snack, Cheez-Its if there were any. But then he had an idea of his own: if he asked Mrs. Merdle about the teacup, maybe he wouldn't have to talk to Edie.

"The walnut table is a beautiful piece, Mrs. Merdle," Arthur said. "Super antique. Also I believe we can offer a very fair price."

"Way to close the sale, Arthur," Dad said. Then, to Mrs. Merdle, "I taught him everything he knows."

Mrs. Merdle smiled. "You've got this store in your veins, Arthur. From both sides of the family."

"Take a look and see what you think." Dad stood up and smiled brightly at Arthur. Arthur translated the smile: "I owe you one, bud."

The walnut table was the same one where Arthur and Veda usually worked on Sunday afternoons. Now he led Mrs. Merdle through the store to its spot in Dining Room Furniture.

"It is lovely," Mrs. Merdle said, "but perhaps a little large. I sold my house, you know. Now I live in a condo."

"Shall I keep an eye out for something smaller?" Arthur asked. "We get new inventory all the time."

"You are so good at customer service, Arthur," Mrs. Merdle said.

Arthur was tired of hearing this but still said, "Thank you." Then, "Uh . . . if you don't mind? I have kind of a funny question for you too."

"Really? And what's that?" Mrs. Merdle asked.

The whole thing—how the teacup had showed up out of nowhere, how Grandpa had said he recognized it, how it was a hangout for the mouse who was haunting him but now Ramona had stolen it—was too much to explain.

So Arthur simplified. "Do you know if Edie used to have a teacup with a dancing bear on it? A chipped teacup, I mean. No saucer."

If Arthur had expected anything, it was that Mrs. Merdle would say no, and he would have to talk to Edie after all. He certainly did not expect what actually happened, which was that Mrs. Merdle suddenly looked sick.

"Are you okay?" Arthur asked.

"Fine," Mrs. Merdle said quickly, but she didn't look fine. "I probably should have eaten lunch, is all. Now." She swallowed. "What about Edie and a teacup? I don't think I remember any teacup. No, I'm sure that I do not."

Arthur shrugged. "Okay. It's just something Edie said to Ramona."

"What did Edie say to Ramona?" Mrs. Merdle asked.

"I don't know exactly," Arthur said. "Just that she used to have this teacup. I can check with Edie if you don't remember."

"Don't do that," Mrs. Merdle said quickly. "It . . . isn't that I don't remember. It's that there is no such teacup."

Not for the first time, Arthur thought, *Grown-ups are weird.*

But weird or not, Mrs. Merdle was a good customer. "Sure, Mrs. Merdle. Absolutely," he said.

"And I don't want you hectoring my granddaughter about this either," she went on.

What is hectoring? Arthur wondered. "Right. I would never do that, Mrs. Merdle," he said.

"Promise me, Arthur."

Arthur didn't think Mrs. Merdle looked insane exactly, just intense. "I will not hector Edie," he said. "I promise."

Color returned to Mrs. Merdle's cheeks. "Excellent," she said. "You forget all about that teacup, Arthur. That teacup does not exist."

Upstairs eating Cheez-Its at the kitchen table, Arthur got out his phone and looked up "hector," which turned out to mean "harass, bully, or intimidate."

I would never harass, bully, or intimidate Edie—or anybody else, either, Arthur thought. *Not even the guys at the lunch table.* And for a fact he was insulted that Mrs. Merdle would say that to him.

On the other hand he might still ask Edie *politely* about the teacup. Because the teacup did exist, whatever Mrs. Merdle said, and now he really wanted to know what the story with it was, and why Mrs. Merdle was acting weird too.

But first he had some questions for his mom.

CHAPTER FORTY-ONE

t was Dad's turn to clean up that night, so after dinner Arthur followed his mom to her office and stood in the doorway as she sat down at her desk and fired up the computer.

"Mom?"

"Oh!" Mom started and spun around in her swivel chair. "You scared me, kiddo!"

"Sorry." Arthur stepped into the room, wiped the bangs out of his eyes.

Mom cocked her head at him. "Do you need a haircut?" she asked.

"No," Arthur said.

"We could take care of those bangs right now," Mom persisted. "I've got scissors in my desk and—"

"No!" Arthur kind of liked his long bangs. "Anyway, don't you have to be, like, a professional to cut hair?"

"Not technically," his mom said. "I mean, scissors meet

hair—*snip, snip*. I guess maybe to do a good job it takes a professional."

"Can we wait, then?" Arthur said.

Mom shrugged. "I guess. Are you okay, though? What do you need? I was just going to get a little work done, but . . ."

Across the room from Mom's desk was a flower-patterned sofa that had come from the store. Arthur sat down on the edge and said, "It's about your book group."

"Uh . . . said no child ever?" Mom said. "What in the world?"

Arthur smiled. "Grandma said basically the same thing yesterday."

"You talked to her about book group too?" Mom's eyebrows approached her hairline.

Arthur plunged ahead. He had thought about how to word this question but hadn't really come up with a solution. "So what I want to know is," he began, "are there any, like, shady characters in your book group?"

Mom didn't answer right away, and Arthur continued. "Not Molly Hart," he said. "And not Sandy Young. And not Susana Malarky, either. I mean, maybe they're shady, but if they are, I don't care. They don't count."

Mom seemed to be too surprised to speak, so Arthur added, "Oh, and not Grandma either."

"What about me? Can I be shady?" Mom asked.

"For a fact, I don't have proof," Arthur said, remembering what Watson had said. "So maybe."

Mom shifted in her chair. Arthur wondered if that was a sign that she was nervous. Could Watson be right? But she was his very own mother!

"Huh," Mom said at last. "Well. I'm a little confused, Arthur. But now I'm wondering, does all this have something to do with Grandma's missing necklace?"

Arthur said, "No!" because the question surprised him, but right away he backtracked. "Maybe? But why would you even ask?"

Could she really be the thief? he wondered.

Mom said, "Arthur, you are not the only one who can put two and two together. I know from Dad that your grandpa thinks Maria's friend Juan might have taken the necklace. It would be like you to try to prove he didn't."

Arthur took a breath, relieved. "Oh good. So you didn't steal it."

"Why would I?" Mom said. "I can borrow it anytime I want."

This answer seemed disappointing. "Is that the only reason?"

"Also because stealing is wrong, Arthur. But as for your question, how about if you define 'shady'?"

Arthur thought for a second. "I guess I mean likely to be a criminal, uh . . . untrustworthy."

"Hmmm," said Mom. "Well, Susana often claims to have read the whole book when it's obvious she didn't, but you said she doesn't count. And I know with certainty that several members keep their library books long after they're due. Your grandma definitely does that, but you said she doesn't count either."

"How many people are even in your book group?" Arthur asked.

"I think the list is around thirty. But we rarely get that many at meetings. Fifteen is more like it," Mom said.

So fifteen suspects, Arthur thought, and then he realized something else. "The shady person I'm thinking of"— he spoke his thoughts out loud—"has to be somebody who was at the meeting on Monday, and it's probably someone who goes to most of the meetings. So do you remember who was there on Monday?"

Mom scrunched up her face, trying to remember. "All

the ones you mentioned already. They're regulars. And Grandma, of course, and me. Oh—and Amy Merdle, which kind of surprised me, since she's getting ready for the Stomp. Besides that, how 'bout if I think back and write them down? The book was short, and short books usually attract better turnouts. But, Arthur, kiddo, I don't think anyone in my book group would steal a necklace. Like I said, it's wrong, but also you'd be so embarrassed if you got caught."

"What if she knew she would never get caught?" Arthur asked.

CHAPTER FORTY-TWO

Arthur got into bed that night and, light still on, studied the list of names his mom had printed out. There were twenty, including Mom and Grandma.

Besides the ones he already knew about, a couple were familiar: Lily Unger, who was a neighbor of Grandma and Grandpa's; and Petra Kessler, who had been Arthur's preschool teacher. Neither one of them seemed shady, but how could he know for sure?

After all, Grandpa thought Juan was shady, just because he was a Latino guy with tattoos.

Maybe I'm asking the wrong question, Arthur thought. *Maybe instead I should be asking* why *someone would steal all that jewelry.*

Except that answer seemed obvious. For money, of course. But didn't the people in the book group already have money?

"Hey, Arthur, good evening." Watson appeared on the bedpost. "Whatcha got there?"

"It's a list," Arthur said, and he explained. "I don't know who stole the jewelry yet," he continued, "but I think Veda and I will find Grandma's necklace tomorrow. I think I know where it is."

"That's just fine, Arthur," Watson said. "You're becoming a detective at last! Now, how 'bout my teacup?"

Arthur laid the list on his bedside table and turned out the light. "I'm working on that, too," he said. "It must be in Ramona's room, but I don't know where."

Arthur didn't explain how Mrs. Merdle had claimed that the teacup didn't exist. He and Watson both knew it did exist, so what was the point?

"Did you try asking Ramona?" Watson asked.

Arthur said, "That won't work," knowing Watson would ask "Why not?" which is exactly what Watson did.

"Because she says the teacup isn't mine, it's Edie's. Only, Edie says Ramona can keep it for now. You know for her friend Bluebell, the cow," Arthur said.

"But Bluebell isn't even real!" Watson protested.

"I know that," Arthur said.

"Why does a cow that's not even real need her own hangout?"

"I dunno, Watson," Arthur said. "First graders like Ramona have crazy ideas. Or anyway, Ramona has crazy ideas. She thinks Bluebell's barn is in her jammie drawer, which . . . wait a sec."

"Jammie drawer," Watson repeated.

"Yeah," said Arthur thoughtfully. Then, "Yeah! I'll get your hangout back tomorrow, Watson. I promise. And I think I'll get my grandma's necklace, too. Only, that's not in Ramona's jammie drawer. It's somewhere else."

When Arthur got up the next morning, no one was around. Mom and Dad must've been at work. As for Ramona, Arthur thought she was at tae kwon do. She had as many activities as Veda. It was hard to keep them all straight.

Arthur fixed a bowl of cereal for breakfast, ate it, and texted Veda.

C u at 1, she texted back.

"Ramona?" Arthur called, just to be sure. When there was no answer, he figured it was time to raid the jammie drawer.

Arthur did not enjoy being sneaky. Being sneaky made

him nervous. Still, sometimes it had to be done. He thought of Watson and, heart thumping, padded toward Ramona's room. The door was ajar, and Arthur bumped it open with his elbow, careful not to use the doorknob. In movies, the police often found fingerprints on the doorknob.

Being in Ramona's room by himself felt pretty strange. Her bed was unmade, the pink sheets in a tangle, and her pajamas were in a tiny heap on the floor. Arthur caught himself thinking, *I shouldn't be here.* He had to remind himself it was her fault in the first place.

Ramona's room, like Arthur's, was large. It took strides to reach the dresser, which was next to the window. In the dresser were five drawers, but which one held jammies? His own he kept in the top drawer, so he pulled that one open first and was startled when it made an awful squeak.

Yikes, I'm gonna get caught! he thought. *Except there's no one here to catch me.*

And no jammies, either. So he tried the next lower one, and the next, carefully pushing each one closed as he went. T-shirts, jeans, shorts, socks, underwear, now and then a crayon or stuffed animal—everything but jammies.

And no teacup, either.

At last he knelt and yanked open the bottom drawer, which also squeaked.

The dancing-bear teacup was right on top. Ramona hadn't even bothered to bury it.

Arthur grabbed the teacup, shoved the drawer shut— *squeak!*—and stood, thrilled to be making his escape.

But when he turned around, his sister was standing in the doorway, wearing her tae kwon do uniform and scowling.

CHAPTER FORTY-THREE

Arthur said, "I thought you were at tae kwon do," which was dumb, but he was too surprised to say anything smarter.

"I was, but now I'm not," Ramona said, "and get out of my room."

"Sure. Fine," Arthur said, and he tried to hold the teacup so she couldn't see it, tried to slip past her out the door.

This did not work.

"Wait," Ramona commanded, stepping sideways to block his exit. "What are you holding? What are you doing in here?"

"Nothing," Arthur said, "and I can't leave if you won't get out of the way."

"You're trying to steal that teacup, aren't you? Give it over." Ramona held out her hand.

Arthur stopped. "No way. For a fact, it's mine, and you stole it from me, and you're not allowed in my room."

"You're not allowed in my room either," Ramona said.

"Good. Fine. I'm leaving!" Arthur tried to get by her again, but she was quick and sturdy. "This is ridiculous, Ramona," Arthur said. "You know it's mine, and you know that you and Edie took it. Why are you being stubborn? Why did you go into my room in the first place?"

Ramona was a lot smaller than Arthur. To compensate she yelled and made her face extra mean. Her dark eyebrows were good for that. "To get a pencil, *okay*?"

Confused, Arthur turned down his volume a notch. "A pencil?" he repeated.

"Yeah!" Ramona said, as loud as ever. "And besides, how did you even know where the teacup was?"

"You said Bluebell's barn is in your jammie drawer, and you stole the teacup for Bluebell, so that's how I knew." Arthur was kind of proud that he'd figured that out.

"Huh," Ramona said, "but anyway the teacup isn't really yours. It's Edie's. Bluebell is just keeping it for her."

Arthur didn't like confrontation. Confrontation was scary, and Arthur wasn't brave. At least, that's how he'd always thought of it. Fighting with Ramona now, though, he wasn't scared. He was more like impatient and wanted to be done.

"Ramona, can we stop fighting for a sec?" he asked.

Ramona looked suspicious. "Why?"

"Because it's boring? Because I have a question?"

"What question?" Ramona still looked suspicious, but she wasn't yelling.

"Where did you get this idea that the teacup belongs to Edie?"

"From *Edie,* duh! She told me."

"What exactly did she tell you?" Arthur said.

"I don't have to tell you that," Ramona said.

"Okay, great," Arthur said. "So, why did you want one of my pencils, anyway?"

Ramona's eyebrows rose and fell. She looked confused.

"You said you wanted a pencil?" Arthur said. "That's why you went into my room, remember?"

"Oh, right," Ramona said. "Because your pencils are sharper than mine, okay? And Edie and I were going to draw. But then we got out the old jewelry instead, and—"

"Hang on a sec." Arthur tried to get by her again, and she blocked him, and he thought *What the heck* and handed over the teacup.

Ramona was so surprised that she fumbled it, but recovered. Then she let him by.

How crazy would it be if the teacup broke? Arthur thought on his way down the hall.

Thirty seconds later he was back in Ramona's room. "Here." He gave her a pencil sharpener, the small boxy plastic kind. "I had an extra. Now your pencils will be sharp too."

Ramona took the sharpener, looked at it as if it were dangerous, and finally said, "Thank you."

"You're welcome," Arthur said. "So, uh . . . what did Edie say? Do you mind telling me? Dad gave me the teacup after I found it in the store. So I don't get—"

"She says she used to play with it, she and Teddy."

"Teddy?" Arthur repeated.

"You know. Her stuffy," Ramona said, "her bear."

"Creative name," Arthur said.

"She and Teddy played tea party," Ramona continued, "with her grandmother. And that was her favorite teacup."

Arthur's turn to be confused. "So . . . according to Edie, it's not actually her teacup—Edie's teacup." He was thinking out loud. "It's Mrs. Merdle's. Right?"

"Whatever," Ramona said. "Anyway, it's not yours."

Arthur shook his head. "This is all wrong, Mo, and I'll tell you why. Mrs. Merdle says she never saw a chipped teacup with a dancing bear. She claims it doesn't exist."

"Well, that's ridiculous," said Ramona. "It does exist 'cause there it is, so Mrs. Merdle is wrong. Sometimes grown-ups are wrong. I hate to tell you, Arthur, but they are."

Arthur sighed. "I know. And it's almost like Mrs. Merdle is lying. But why would she bother to lie about a teacup?"

CHAPTER FORTY-FOUR

By the time Arthur left Ramona, they were getting along okay. He had told her what Grandpa said about the teacup—how it disappeared long ago, then came back. She had told him it was okay with Bluebell if he borrowed it. This did not seem like a good time to point out to Ramona that Bluebell was imaginary. Instead he returned to his room and put the cup on the shelf by the Sherlock Holmes books.

"Watson?" he said. "Look what I brought you."

Arthur was hoping Watson would be grateful that he had gotten her hangout back, that she'd tell him "Good job." He was also thinking he'd tell the mouse what Ramona had told him about Edie and Teddy and the teacup—see if Watson had any ideas about why Mrs. Merdle might be lying.

But Watson did not answer, didn't seem to be around.

So now what? Arthur thought.

It was a couple of minutes before noon, an hour

before he was supposed to meet Veda. He could do some homework. Or read *King Arthur.* But really—there wasn't enough time for either of those, was there?

He looked out the window, and his thoughts turned back to detecting, back to the pearl necklace. He was pretty sure he knew where it was; that's where he and Veda were going on their bikes. Unfortunately, he would only be able to see the necklace, not get it back right away to give to his grandmother.

Unless . . .

. . . he requested backup.

Arthur picked up his phone, looked through his contacts, found what he was looking for, started to send a text, stopped. Maybe this was what his mom would call "inappropriate"? Like, too big an ask?

Plus, maybe if he had help, he wouldn't get all the credit for being a good detective, for solving the case.

On the other hand it would be so much better actually to hand back Grandma's pearl necklace, not just tell her he knew where it was. He pictured it like the end of a Sherlock Holmes story, the part where Sherlock tells everyone how he figured everything out. If Arthur had the necklace, that scene would be way cooler.

Arthur counted the cars going by on the busy street outside. When he got to ten—five blue, three black, one white, and one gray—he made his decision.

A couple of minutes later he sent the text.

Almost instantly he got a reply: **How nice to hear from you, Arthur. I would be happy to.**

Arthur's bike was a red three-speed. It came from the store, of course. It was a little too big, but he was used to it, and at 12:59 p.m. he walked it out into the parking lot. Veda was there already, riding in circles and figure eights, waiting for him.

"How do you know Juan didn't take the pearls?" she asked, not bothering to say hi, not bothering to stop. "And can you please tell Officer Bernstein that?"

"Officer Bernstein," Arthur repeated. "Wait—what? Why?" He tugged on his helmet, buckled it, and had a terrible thought. "Oh no—did Juan get arrested?"

Veda shook her head. "The only evidence is what your grandpa says, and that's not real evidence. I mean, right? But my mom is upset. For now she won't even let Juan work for her. She says it might look bad to the customers."

"That's not good," Arthur said.

"Sí, claro," Veda said. "She had to turn down a job at this lady Mrs. Hart's house because she didn't have enough cleaners, and Mrs. Hart is a regular."

"Molly Hart?"

"With red hair, that one," Veda said. "Do you know her?"

"From the store," Arthur said, "and she's in my mom's book group."

Veda nodded. "I think Mom cleans for everybody in that book group."

"Huh, that's funny," said Arthur, thinking how all of a sudden this book group was everywhere. But then he got a bad feeling. "Veda," he said, "so would you say Juan cleans for a lot of people in that book group, then? He works a lot for your mom, right?"

Veda shrugged. "Yeah, maybe. Why?"

The bad feeling got worse. "I might have to sit down a sec," Arthur said, and he did—right on the asphalt.

"Arthur! Get up! Are you okay?"

Arthur didn't answer right away. One reason why Grandpa thought Juan had stolen the necklace was that Juan had been in their house cleaning right before Grandma had hosted book group. Arthur wasn't sure when Juan had started cleaning for Veda's mother. But what if that was a while ago? What if he had been in other book group members' houses too? Then maybe their jewelry hadn't disappeared at meetings like Arthur had thought.

What if Grandpa was right, and the thief really was Juan?

CHAPTER FORTY-FIVE

Veda jumped off her bike and let it fall, then bent down next to Arthur. "Get up right now!" she said. "You're scaring me!"

"Way to be supportive, Darth," he said weakly.

"Whatever works." She yanked his arm.

"Ow!" Arthur got to his feet slowly. "I'm okay," he said, "except for my arm, I mean. I just thought of something, is all."

"So stop thinking and let's go. I am a busy person, Arthur." Veda jumped onto her bike and started riding in circles again. "So, where are we going?"

Arthur adjusted his helmet, then put his hands on the handlebars. "Jumper Jewelers on Pearl Street."

Veda shook her head, like *Whatever,* but before she could actually say the word, the back door of the store opened and Ramona came out.

"Hey, wait a sec! Wait! Dad says you have to watch me

this afternoon. Ballet's canceled and he has to go somewhere."

Arthur's first thought was, *Unbelievable,* and his second was, *No way,* and his third was, *Maybe this means we're not supposed to do this at all.*

Arthur didn't say any of that, though. He said, "Why?"

"He has to meet Mom somewhere. So, where are we going? Hi, Veda."

"Hi, Mo."

"Is there, like, an *emergency*?" Arthur wondered if he was supposed to be worrying about something besides what he was worrying about already.

Ramona shrugged. "I don't think so. He wasn't freaking out."

Arthur saw this for himself when Dad came out the door a second later.

"So, how come I'm in charge of Ramona?" Arthur asked. "Veda and I were on our way, uh . . ." He realized he couldn't explain, not yet. Luckily, Dad wasn't paying that much attention.

"Yeah, sorry." Dad examined the keys he'd taken from his pocket. "And thanks for entertaining your sister. Grandma sent an SOS, something to do with that fundraiser thing tonight. Prairie dogs, right? It seems they need a truck, and we've got one. I'll be back in a flash, but in the meantime . . ."

"Can't Ramona entertain herself?" Arthur argued. "Or isn't Randolph—"

Dad looked up from his keys. "Bud, could you please just—"

"We got this," Veda said. Then she looked at Arthur. "We can take the bus."

Ramona was delighted with this idea, and ten minutes later they were at the bus stop, waiting. The bus from North Boulder to downtown is called the Hop. Arthur had ridden it maybe twice, and Ramona never had. When it came, Veda turned out to be a pro—showed Arthur how to use his phone to pay, and told Ramona she didn't have to because she wasn't old enough.

"I should pay. I take up space too." Ramona sounded insulted.

"If it makes you feel better, you can stand up," Arthur said.

"I can? Cool!" Ramona smiled and looked out the window, like she was on a ride at a theme park.

It's not only grown-ups that are weird, Arthur thought. *First graders are too.*

"So what is it we're doing again?" Veda asked on the way.

"I'll explain," Arthur said, "if we find the necklace."

"What necklace?" Ramona asked. "Grandma's necklace?"

Arthur ignored her.

"So we're looking for a necklace at Jumper Jewelers," Veda said.

"Yes," Arthur said.

"And if we find it, it proves Juan is innocent," Veda said.

"What necklace?" Ramona repeated.

"Yes," Arthur said. "That is, I think. I hope."

Only, what if instead it proves that Juan did it?

"And that's all you're going to tell me?" Veda said.

"For right now," Arthur said. "Or else for about ten years. Because if it's not there, it will be ten years till I'm not too embarrassed to ever bring it up."

CHAPTER FORTY-SIX

The bus dropped Arthur, Veda, and Ramona off at the Pearl Street Mall, which is the cute part of Boulder—the part tourists see when they take a break from hiking and climbing. Jumper Jewelers is on the mall part of Pearl, the part closed to cars and paved with brick instead of asphalt. Most of the buildings on the mall are at least a hundred years old.

Arthur had been to some of the restaurants there before. He'd been to all three ice cream places and both candy stores, but he had never been to Jumper Jewelers—or any jewelry store, come to think of it. Stepping off the bus, he was glad Veda was with him.

Then there was Ramona.

Oh well. It wasn't likely she'd mess anything up. He doubted she'd even talk.

The store was a block away from the bus stop. Before they went inside, they checked out the windows, shiny with diamonds, opals, rubies, and topazes set in gold, platinum, and silver. At Universal Trash, all the jewelry was packed tight in a single glass case. Here in these windows it was spread out, each piece on its own, each one announcing how special it was.

Veda called the windows "tasteful," and added, "Can we get ice cream after? If we find the necklace, it'll be celebrating. And if we don't, it'll make us feel better."

"Mango, please," Ramona said.

"Did you bring money?" Arthur asked his sister.

Veda said, "I'll treat," before Ramona could answer, and right away Arthur felt bad.

"No, I will," he said. "You're doing me a favor, Darth."

"What about me?" Ramona wanted to know.

"I am doing Dad a favor," Arthur said. "But I guess I can buy you ice cream."

Ramona said, "Mango, please," then looked up at him. "Your face is funny, you know."

Arthur was feeling a flutter in his belly. This could all go super wrong, he realized. "Not as funny as yours, Ramona. Come on. Let's go."

Veda pushed open the glass entrance door. Inside were three customers, two of them looking around on their own, one talking to a saleswoman who was wearing a skirt and blazer. They were speaking quietly, as if jewelry deserved respect. In fact, the whole store felt that way, almost like church.

"Good afternoon." A blond saleswoman wearing nice clothes and pink lipstick approached them. "May I help you?" Her voice was friendly, and her smile seemed sincere. *Good at customer service,* Arthur thought.

"Yes." Arthur squared his shoulders, went all customer-service himself. "My friend and I would like to see the vintage jewelry."

"Your friend and you *and* your sister," Ramona said.

The saleswoman smiled like *Isn't she cute?*—didn't see Ramona scowl and stick her tongue out. "If you'll follow me," the saleswoman said. "We have some lovely pieces. Are you looking for a gift?"

Arthur, Veda, and Ramona followed her toward a counter near the back of the store. Unlike the other displays, the tasteful ones, this one shone abundantly. It was not packed quite as tight as the case at Universal Trash, but almost. If his grandmother's necklace was even there, finding it was going to be like finding Waldo. Arthur expected they would have to study the jewelry piece by piece by piece for a long time.

Or not.

Grandma's necklace was on the top shelf, displayed in an open black velvet box. It was the emerald clasp that gave it away.

"Hey—that's Grandma's pearl necklace," Ramona said. "What's it doing here?"

"Hello, Arthur. Hello, Veda. Hello, Ramona, too. Good to see you all."

So much had happened since Arthur had requested backup that, till that moment, he'd forgotten. Now he turned toward the familiar voice and blinked.

"How can I be of service?" Officer Bernstein asked. He was wearing regular clothes, not his uniform. Arthur guessed he wasn't working.

"Hey, Officer Bernstein," Ramona said. "Look at that— it's my grandmother's stolen necklace. Arthur found it!"

"Stolen?" The blond saleswoman half choked on the word.

"Don't worry." Ramona seemed to feel bad for her. "I bet you didn't steal it, right?"

"I? Well, of course not, but—"

"Did you see who brought it in to sell?" Ramona asked. "What did he look like? That's the thief, probably—don't you think so, Officer Bernstein? Or maybe Arthur knows who the thief is already. My brother doesn't look like it, but he's smart sometimes."

Arthur was horrified. He hadn't expected Ramona to talk at all! *I will never bring her anywhere again,* he was thinking, and he wanted to apologize to the saleswoman.

But before he could, the woman spoke—sounding a little shaky. "I . . . I don't remember her name, only that she was wearing those funky *Lion King* earrings. . . ."

CHAPTER FORTY-SEVEN

n the end Officer Bernstein bought the ice cream. And after that he explained why the police hadn't found the missing necklace and returned it to Grandma already.

"Naturally," he said, "we at the BPD reach out to both Jumper Jewelers and Universal Trash anytime we get a report of stolen jewelry. In this particular case, though, no report."

Ramona said, "You mean my grandparents didn't call nine-one-one and say, 'Hey, our necklace is missing!'?" Ramona was sitting on an iron-and-wood bench outside the ice cream store eating her mango cone. Veda (strawberry sundae) was on her left and Arthur (double chocolate cone) was on her right. Officer Bernstein had a bench to himself, facing them. He wasn't exactly eating his kid-size marshmallow sundae. He was more like watching it melt.

"Yes, more or less. That is, they didn't file a report," Officer Bernstein said. "As I believe you know, your grandfather had his own particular theory that he wished us to investigate. But the necklace belonged to your grandmother. I believe it was she who chose not to report it."

"So is that why you couldn't take the necklace right now?" Arthur had been disappointed. He'd known that plain old Arthur Popper, private citizen, age eleven, wouldn't be able to convince anybody at the jewelry store to hand him the necklace. But he figured a sworn officer of the law like Officer Bernstein could convince them. Then he, Arthur, would return it to Grandma, and she would say he was wonderful—good at something besides customer service, even—and he would feel a glowing sense of accomplishment.

That was why he had texted Officer Bernstein in the first place.

But, like a lot of his good ideas lately, this one hadn't worked out.

On the way to the ice cream store, Officer Bernstein had explained that once he got the paperwork from the BPD, he could go back and interview the store manager, get a description of the suspect, and probably get the pearl necklace, too.

But paperwork took time, and this was the weekend.

It would probably be Tuesday at least before he could go back to Jumper Jewelers.

Ramona, Veda, and Arthur finished their ice cream. Officer Bernstein ate his in three bites. Then he contemplated the empty cup, tossed it into the trash, sighed, and offered the kids a ride home.

Ramona was excited. "In the police car? With the siren?"

"Just my Prius, I'm afraid," said Officer Bernstein sadly.

Even without a siren the ride back was quick. On the way, Veda didn't say much, Arthur noticed. Then he realized she hadn't said much when they'd been eating ice cream either. Was she mad at him? He hadn't gotten the necklace or identified the thief. She must have been disappointed too.

Officer Bernstein let the three of them out in the parking lot at the store and waved as he drove away. Ramona had swimming lessons, so she disappeared upstairs to change. Arthur figured Veda had to get home, so he turned to tell her goodbye . . . and got a big surprise. Right there in the parking lot in front of all the cars and everyone—she gave him a huge hug.

"Wait . . . what?" Arthur was too freaked out to move.

Except for that time when she'd slugged him, Veda had never touched him before. "What's wrong? Are you okay?"

Veda let go and looked into his face. She was grinning. "I'm just happy!" she said. "And grateful, too. Muchas gracias, Arturo!"

Arthur was confused. "But I didn't get the necklace back," he said. "And we still don't know who stole it. Or any of the other jewelry, either."

"You idiot!" Veda said, and Arthur felt better. This was more like the usual Veda. "You proved Juan *didn't* steal it."

"I did?" Arthur said.

"Well, *yeah*! I mean, unless Juan dressed up like a woman and wore lion earrings when he took the necklace to Jumper. Right?"

"Yeah, you're right," he said slowly, remembering what the saleswoman had said. "I don't see Juan wearing lion earrings. I mean, skulls or something. But not lions."

"Of course not!" Veda said. "And Officer Bernstein was right there when she said it too. So he knows Juan didn't do it. I can't wait to tell Mamá!"

Afraid of getting hugged again, Arthur stepped back. "You're welcome," he said, "and Juan is welcome too. But there's still one problem. We still don't know who did it."

CHAPTER FORTY-EIGHT

Arthur was glad Juan didn't do it.

He was glad Veda was happy.

He was even glad, he guessed, that eventually Officer Bernstein would find out from Jumper Jewelers who'd stolen the necklace—and probably all the other jewelry, too.

But for a fact, in spite of all he was glad about, Arthur felt bummed.

He had expected by this afternoon to have that whole glowing sense of etc., but no. The mystery remained a mystery. He, Arthur, had not solved it. He wasn't a good detective after all.

And what now?

He thought of checking in at the store to see if they needed help. He even thought of doing homework or reading *King Arthur*.

Then he had a better idea. At school they had learned

how exercise is good for the chemicals in your brain. He would walk around the lake. Maybe that would improve the chemicals.

In Boulder people used to take blue sky for granted. But lately there had been lots of wildfires nearby, and the wildfires sometimes sent their smoke toward town. That meant the blue sky, when there was blue sky like today, seemed special. Setting out across the parking lot and onto the trail, Arthur was glad for blue sky.

Soon—was it brain chemicals?—he realized that, looked at one way, the BPD paperwork was his friend. It gave him until Tuesday, three days if Officer Bernstein was right, to solve the mystery himself.

But how?

Basically, the question came down to this: Who was the woman with the lion earrings? The thief, right? And the thief was also, probably, someone in the book group, and that meant . . .

I should ask Mom and Grandma if anyone in their book group ever wears lion earrings.

Duh! It was obvious. In fact, he would've turned around right then, except that both Mom and Grandma were busy with that Stomp fundraiser. He would probably have to wait till tomorrow at least to talk to either one of them.

Meanwhile Arthur tried to remember the names on the book group list his mom had given him, tried to think if any of those names would belong to a person who really, really loved lions.

When this process got him nowhere, he stopped walking and took a deep breath. The air smelled like the lake, watery green. The trail wound among purple wildflowers and through a village of prairie dog burrows. As he watched, three of the critters sat up on their haunches and watched him back. High in the sky, black turkey vultures wheeled. Arthur looked up at them and squinted. One of them, soaring on its own, might even have been an eagle.

Arthur moved on. He was glad for nature. He was a little less bummed. Still, detecting was hard work. Maybe he should go back to customer service.

The kitchen clock said 4:29 when Arthur got home.

"Where've ya been, kiddo?" his dad asked. "Up to no good as usual?"

Arthur wanted to tell his dad about the necklace, Officer Bernstein, and Veda—except that would take a few minutes, and his dad was obviously in a hurry. "Not exactly," Arthur said. "Are you dressed for tonight already?"

Dad was wearing real pants, not jeans or khakis, a button-up shirt, and a tie, even. The tie was dark green with pictures of red squirrels on it.

"The social event of the season!" Dad said. "How do I look?"

"Isn't that a Christmas tie?" Arthur asked.

"Probably," Dad said, "but it's brand-new."

"And those aren't prairie dogs; they're squirrels," Arthur said.

"Close cousins of prairie dogs, right?" Dad said.

Arthur shrugged. "I guess?" He wondered if prairie dogs were cousins with mice, too. "So what time is this thing?"

"Not till seven," Dad said, "but I have to go retrieve the truck in a few minutes, which, uh . . . brings me to something else I have to tell you."

"Yeah?" Arthur realized he was hungry. "Can I have a snack?"

Dad said sure and actually got the good cookies down from the high shelf. Arthur did not mention his double chocolate cone. "So the thing is," Dad continued, "you know your mom and I, and your grandma, we're all going to this event tonight."

Arthur popped a whole cookie into his mouth. "Uh-huh," he said, chewing, and then he realized his dad looked serious. "What's wrong?"

"So we can't leave you and Ramona home alone," Dad said. "I mean, obviously."

"Not obviously." Arthur was getting suspicious. "I'm old enough. Didn't I take the bus downtown today?"

But Dad was shaking his head. "That was daytime, Arthur. Soon maybe we'll let you stay alone at night, but not quite yet. So, the thing is . . . Grandpa is coming over."

"Wait, what? Why isn't *he* going to the Prairie Dog Stomp?" Arthur asked.

"Your grandpa," Dad said slowly, "is not big on social events. He would rather spend time with his beloved grandchildren. You should be honored."

Arthur frowned. "Right."

Now Dad was getting annoyed. "Look, kiddo," he said, "I know Grandpa can be a little difficult, but he cares about you, and—"

"He thinks Juan stole Grandma's necklace!" Arthur said. "And Juan didn't! I have proof! That's where Mo and I were this afternoon, getting proof. Officer Bernstein knows too."

Dad nodded, obviously distracted. "Great," he said. "Good. I'm sure you'll tell me about it tomorrow. Meanwhile—"

"But, Dad—" Arthur started.

Dad shook his head, raised his hand. "I am so sorry, kiddo, but I don't have time," he said. "Now, for tonight can you just be *pleasant* to your grandpa? Don't mention anything about the necklace or about Juan. Nothing controversial, right? Tomorrow you can tell me all about it."

CHAPTER FORTY-NINE

Dad left to get the truck, and soon after, Mom came home with Ramona and two bags of McDonald's for dinner.

Arthur couldn't believe his luck. Ice cream, cookies, and fast food in one day?

But Ramona complained. "Fast food is unhealthy, Mama. We learned it in school."

"I'll eat your fries, then," Arthur said. He reached for one, and Ramona batted his hand. "I didn't say I didn't want it."

"It's just one night, and you'll live," Mom said. "Now, if you'll excuse me, I've got to get ready."

"Mom?" Arthur said. "Can I just ask a quick question? About your book group?"

"Arthur, I love you, but I've got to take a shower and do my hair and all that. Tomorrow, okay? I promise."

• • •

By the time Grandpa opened the mudroom door, Arthur and Ramona had crumpled their McDonald's bags and thrown them away. Grandpa was grinning.

"Hi, Grandpa," Ramona greeted him. "Are you okay?"

"Yes, I'm okay," Grandpa said, still grinning. "Why wouldn't I be?"

Ramona stared for a few seconds. "It's just that your cheeks look kind of achy. Are your cheeks achy?"

"No!" Grandpa's grin slipped. "Why would you say that?"

Ramona nodded. "That's better. You look more like yourself."

Grandpa snorted, erased the grin altogether. "Your grandmother suggested I should be more *good-humored* around you two." He looked from Ramona to Arthur. "But it didn't work, so fine. Never mind."

Mom came in. Earlier she had been wearing her oldest jeans and a T-shirt. Now she was transformed, wearing her nice green dress, gold high heels, and makeup. The pearl necklace would have looked good, Arthur thought.

"Thanks for doing this, Dad," Mom said. "I know they'll be no trouble. Right, you guys? You will do everything you can to get along?"

Arthur really wanted to say something about Juan and the necklace, but he guessed he had to wait. "Okay," he said unhappily.

And Ramona said, "Of course, Mama," in her most annoying perfect-child voice.

"Great," Mom said. "We won't be super late. I have a lot to get done tomorrow."

After she left, Arthur, Ramona, and Grandpa stood around listening to the sound of her footsteps fading on the stairs. Finally, when it got quiet, Grandpa asked, "So I guess you two probably go to bed early, right?"

"Not that early," Ramona said.

"Oh," Grandpa said. "But I guess you're pretty self-sufficient, right?"

Ramona looked at Arthur. "What does 'self-sufficient' mean?"

Arthur blinked. Usually Ramona didn't admit when she didn't know a word. He was surprised she had asked him, was even a little bit pleased. "'Take care of ourselves,'" he told her.

"Oh?" Ramona said. "So, yeah, I guess. But sometimes Dad plays a game with me. Or Mom reads me a book." She shrugged. "Would you like to read me a book, Grandpa?"

"Depends on the book," Grandpa said.

"*Little House on the Prairie*?" Ramona said.

Grandpa put a finger down his throat—the universal sign for *Gag me.* Arthur cracked up. He didn't like the Little House books either.

"What are you reading, Arthur?" Grandpa asked.

"*King Arthur.* Sort of," Arthur said.

"Are you, now?" Grandpa nodded thoughtfully. "That gives me an idea. You kids ever heard of the Holy Grail?"

CHAPTER FIFTY

The next morning Dad was making coffee when Arthur went into the kitchen. "Where's Mom?" Arthur asked.

Dad yawned. "Still asleep."

Arthur felt bursting with news to tell. Juan was innocent! They'd found the necklace at Jumper Jewelers! It wasn't just the necklace that was missing; there was other jewelry too!

But before he could say any of this, Ramona came in, and she was bursting with questions.

Like, was there a kind of berry called "elderberry," and if there was, did it smell bad? How sharp were rabbits' teeth really? And if a sword cut off somebody's arms and legs, would they still be alive?

Dad had not done anything about breakfast. His face was squinty, as if the light were bright, even though it wasn't.

"Do elderberries smell bad?" Ramona repeated her question.

Very carefully Dad poured coffee from the carafe into a mug and took a sip. Then he sat down at the table.

Ramona leaned close, her face just inches from her dad's. *"Why won't you talk to me?"*

Dad cringed and closed his eyes. "Elderberries, you said?" He opened his eyes. "And sharp teeth?"

"Also cut-off arms and legs," Arthur added helpfully.

Dad nodded. "I think I understand. You and Grandpa watched a movie, didn't you? *Monty Python and the Holy Grail.* I believe that's one of his favorites."

Dad took a couple more sips before answering the questions: He had never smelled elderberries; real rabbits' teeth weren't sharp, as far as he knew; and a person whose arms and legs had been cut off would probably die . . . unless they got medical treatment fast.

"So the movie was all lies?" Ramona said.

"It's supposed to be funny," Arthur said.

"It was *kind* of funny," Ramona said, "especially the cartoon parts. But the blood was yucky."

"And once, Grandpa sent us out because it was inappropriate," Arthur added.

"Maybe don't mention any of this to your mom," Dad said.

"Where is Mom?" Ramona asked.

Dad said, "She's sleeping in," and got to his feet. "Can you guys get your own breakfast? I need to go downstairs and open up the store."

"But, Dad," Arthur protested. "I want to tell you about Juan and—"

"Maybe if the store isn't too busy, you can tell me later?" Coffee clutched in his hand, Dad headed out and down the stairs.

Ramona looked at her brother and snorted. "What's the point in even *having* parents?"

Arthur said, "I'll get you cereal, Mo."

"I want pancakes," Ramona said.

Arthur wiped his bangs out of his eyes. "Ramona?"

"Okay, *fine*. Cereal," she said. "But put sugar on it, okay?"

Arthur got out bowls, spoons, cereal, milk, and sugar.

"I dreamed about the movie," Ramona told him. "Only the Grail in my dream wasn't gold the way King Arthur's was. It looked like Edie's teacup."

Arthur set Ramona's cereal in front of her, then sat

down himself. "Did King Arthur get the Grail in your dream?" In the movie he didn't. In fact, he and the knights never even saw the real thing. It was one frustration after another. Thinking of detecting, Arthur could relate.

"That part was weird too," Ramona said. "Mixed-up. Sometimes Arthur was the guy in the movie and sometimes Arthur was you."

"A lot of dreams are mixed-up like that," Arthur said.

"I've had dreams before, Arthur," Ramona said. "Duh."

"Duh back," Arthur said, and the two of them finished their cereal.

"Maybe the teacup *is* your holy grail," Ramona said, handing over her bowl. "I mean, it's a cup, and a grail is also a cup. I learned that from the movie."

"The teacup isn't gold, though, or valuable." Arthur put his bowl and Ramona's in the sink. "Plus it's more found than lost."

"So after somebody finds the Grail, like, whether they're a king or not, then what are they supposed to do?" Ramona asked. "Search for something else?"

Arthur thought for a minute. "Yes," he said finally. "That is just what they should do."

CHAPTER FIFTY-ONE

And that, more or less, was what Arthur was going to do too. If his grail was the teacup, it was safely on its shelf. But he still was searching for something, the identity of the jewel thief.

And he had to hurry.

Either tomorrow or the next day, Officer Bernstein would get the paperwork he needed from the BPD. Then he would go to the jewelry store to retrieve Grandma's necklace and question witnesses. It was totally unfair, and totally true, that Officer Bernstein wouldn't have to be clever or smart or a good detective to figure out who the thief was. Since he was a police officer, the people at Jumper would plain old tell him who'd brought in the necklace just as soon as he asked.

Arthur wasn't so lucky. If he was going to prove himself as a detective, he needed to be clever, smart, and efficient, too.

"Mo?" He looked at his little sister. "Can you do me a favor? Mom's still asleep, right?"

"Yeah, I think," Ramona said. "What's the favor?"

"Sneak into Mom's room and look in her jewelry box and see if she has any earrings shaped like lions."

Arthur had expected the sneaking idea to appeal to Ramona, and it did. "You think Mom took Grandma's necklace to Jumper Jewelers? You think Mom's a *thief*?" Ramona didn't seem upset about that, more like excited.

Meanwhile Arthur felt his face turn red. He hadn't expected his little sister, who was only in first grade, to figure stuff out so quickly. "Well, not . . . I mean . . . of course not. But I have to eliminate her as a suspect. That's something detectives do."

"A suspect!" Ramona repeated. "Cool!" But then her expression changed. "Arthur, if Mom had earrings shaped like lions, then we would've seen them."

"Not necessarily," Arthur said. "Maybe she only wears them when she's in disguise."

Disguise sounded even better to Ramona. "Be right back!" she said. "And I'll be as quiet as a mouse."

Arthur folded his hands and clenched his jaw. *Please*

don't let her wake Mom up. Please don't let her wake Mom up. Please don't let—

"Ramona!" Mom's voice was a squeal. "What in the world?"

Arthur spent the next several minutes thinking about what an idiot he was. Sure, he was in a hurry, but Mom almost always worked on Sunday. He should have just waited till she was at work. And why hadn't he asked Watson for help? Watson was smaller than Ramona and quieter. She could've sneaked in and rummaged through Mom's jewelry box, no problem.

But Ramona had been there in the kitchen, and Arthur had wanted to do something right away, and . . . he was an idiot.

At last Arthur heard footsteps in the hall, and then Ramona came into the kitchen with Mom right behind her. Mom's hair looked smashed, and her eyelids drooped. She was wearing an ugly red-and-green bathrobe.

"You're not in trouble," Ramona told Arthur. "But Mom does have a question."

"Of course I'm not in trouble. I didn't do anything," Arthur said, playing dumb. "You're the one who should be in trouble, Ramona. That is, if anyone should be."

Mom looked at Arthur. "Why is it you think I'm a jewel thief?" she asked. "Oh, and a master of disguise, too."

"I don't!" Arthur silently vowed revenge against his little sister.

"So why did you send Ramona to look for lion earrings in my jewelry box?" Mom asked.

Arthur gave up. "Is there anything you *didn't* tell her?" he asked Ramona.

"I can't help it if I'm an honest person," Ramona said.

"Ha!" Arthur said. "What about the other day when you and Edie—"

"Enough." Mom collapsed into a chair. "Did your father leave any coffee?"

Maybe Arthur couldn't help being an honest person himself, because after Mom microwaved some coffee, he explained about Jumper Jewelers and Officer Bernstein and even the BPD paperwork.

"So Juan didn't steal the necklace," he concluded, "no matter what Grandpa says."

"And we didn't tell Grandpa about it either," Ramona added, "because you and Dad said we were supposed to try to get along with him. So instead we watched this scary, inappropriate movie with lots of blood about King Arthur."

"'Your mother was a hamster, and your father smelt of elderberries,'" Mom quoted from the movie.

"Yeah, that one," Ramona said.

"So, Arthur," Mom continued, "as I said before, I am not a thief. And besides that, I don't own and never have owned lion earrings. But if it'll make you feel better, you can look through my jewelry box. Half the stuff in it just—"

"Sits around." Arthur finished the sentence for her.

Mom blinked. "Uh . . . right," she said at last. "But why are you looking for lion earrings? I don't get it."

"I have reason to believe," Arthur said, trying to sound as much like a real detective as possible, "that the thief sometimes wears lion earrings. Can you think of anyone in your book group who has a pair like that?"

Mom closed her eyes. At first Arthur thought she was thinking, but then her eyes stayed shut.

"Mama!" Ramona bumped her shoulder. "Wake up!"

Mom opened her eyes, looked around. "Lion earrings," she said.

"Right, Mom. I guess it was a good party, huh?" Arthur said.

Mom nodded. "We got home very late. Practically everyone I know was there. Oh, and my book group was quite interested in your detecting, Arthur. They were very complimentary."

At first Arthur thought he'd misunderstood. His mom was a smart person, a lawyer. For sure she would never reveal to suspects that they *were* suspects.

Would she?

CHAPTER FIFTY-TWO

Arthur tried to make his voice calm. "Mom?" he said. "You aren't saying you told people in your book group that Grandma's necklace was stolen and I asked you for that list, right? I mean, it was a list of people *in your book group*."

Mom blinked. "Um, actually . . . I guess maybe I might've?"

"Mom!" Arthur said.

And even Ramona shook her head and said, "Mom." She sounded disappointed.

"But, kiddo"—Mom leaned toward her son—"I've known all these people for years, and—"

Arthur was so agitated, he bounced up from his chair. "What difference does that make? Like I told you, I think one of them is a thief!"

At least he hadn't mentioned the other stolen jewelry. Like everyone else, Mom thought this was only about the necklace.

Mom sagged back, rested her head in her hand. "I'm sorry, kiddo," she said. "It was late. I guess I wasn't thinking clearly."

Arthur forced himself to sit back down. *Damage control,* he thought. That was something else he'd heard in a movie. It meant "accept that a bad thing has happened; try to make it as un-bad as possible." He took a deep breath and let it out. "Who exactly did you tell?"

"No one *shady*, if that's what you mean." Now Mom sounded snippy. When Arthur didn't reply, she continued, "Lizzie was there, and Petra. Uh . . . Suzanne—do you know her? Very nice woman, always suggests terrible books. Molly's little boy was sick, so she didn't go. I mean, it wasn't my *whole* book group, Arthur. Not *all* of your suspects."

"Okay," Arthur said. "I'm sorry I got mad. I was just surprised. I would really like to figure out who the thief is. I would really like to see if I'm any good at detecting."

"I understand, honey," Mom said. "And I'm sorry. And—oh, Amy was there too, I think. We were kind of standing in a circle by the punch."

"What about the lion earrings?" Ramona asked, and for once Arthur was grateful to his sister. He'd been distracted, and he almost forgot.

Mom shook her head. "I can't think of anyone in my book group who wears animal jewelry like that at all—oh, except for Amy Merdle. Those prairie dogs of hers."

"A prairie dog is not a lion, Mom," Ramona pointed out.

"Thanks, honey." Mom closed her eyes again. "I knew that."

few minutes later Arthur was in his room getting dressed when he heard Watson's small, pleasant voice.

"Good morning, Arthur." She was back in the chipped dancing-bear teacup—Arthur's very own grail—pink tail drooped over the rim. "I'm glad to have my hangout back. It's just as cozy as ever."

Arthur realized he hadn't seen Watson the night before, and he explained how he'd found the teacup exactly where they'd thought it would be. He was hoping Watson would say "Good job" or something like that, "Thank you," at least.

Instead she said, "And do you know who stole it in the first place? Do you know who brought it to the store?"

Arthur tugged a Scooby-Doo T-shirt over his head and wiped his bangs out of his eyes. He was annoyed. "Look, Watson," he said. "I got it back for you, okay? And I'm working on the rest. Isn't that enough for now? Can't you for once be grateful?"

"Sor-*reee*," Watson said. "Sheesh. Can't a mouse ask a question around here?"

Arthur sighed. "It's just that I thought I was about to solve the mystery of the missing jewelry, too, and it's not working out at all. For a fact, I want to feel that glowing sense of accomplishment, the one you're always talking about."

Watson's small voice got smaller. "I'm sorry, Arthur," she said. "And thank you for bringing back my hangout. I am grateful. And you seem a bit, uh . . . peevish this morning? Did you go to bed awfully late?"

"I did, actually," he said, and he told Watson about Grandpa and the movie.

"That explains it, then," Watson said, "and, if you don't mind my asking, is there anything new on the detecting front?"

"Oh right—I have to catch you up!" he said and sat down on the edge of the bed. Watson was a good audience. She squeaked happily when Arthur told him Juan was innocent and probably Mom was too. She scratched her ears fiercely when Arthur said Officer Bernstein might solve the case before he, Arthur, had a chance to.

"We can't let that happen!" Watson said.

"But I don't know what to do next," Arthur complained.

"You've got one new clue," Watson said, "the saleswoman's comment about your suspect—the person wearing lion earrings. Remember back to the jewelry store. What *exactly* did she say?"

Arthur didn't think remembering would help. But without a better idea, he gave it a try—lay back on his bed, put his feet up over the headboard, and pictured Jumper Jewelers the afternoon before. "Like I told you already," he said, "the saleswoman told us a woman brought in the necklace, and she had on lion earrings." Then he paused. Was that exactly what the saleswoman had said? "You know what, Watson—I mean, not that it matters—but she said the person was wearing 'funky *Lion King* earrings'—*Lion King,* like the movies. Do you know those movies?"

"Of course I do, Arthur," Watson said. "As I've told you before, mice pay attention. Those movies are the ones starring meerkats."

Arthur twisted his head so he could look at Watson. "Wait, what?"

"The ones that star Timon, the meerkat, and his friends

and relations," Watson said. "I mean, I know there's some lions and warthogs and so on, but the star is clearly Timon. Ask any mouse—any rat, even—and they'll tell you."

Arthur thought of his dad's confusion over the squirrels on the tie he wore to the Prairie Dog Stomp. Squirrels were not prairie dogs. As for meerkats, were they even rodents? Were prairie dogs? He wasn't sure, but he guessed he saw a family resemblance, and he laughed.

"You're ridiculous, Watson," he said. "If the movies are about meerkats, why is the title *Lion King*?"

"I've always wondered the same thing," Watson said.

Arthur laughed, decided not to argue. Anyway, who didn't like Timon? For fun he tried to picture what meerkat earrings would look like, and . . . just like that, all of a sudden, he knew who'd stolen Grandma's necklace, and the other jewelry, too, and probably, long ago, a certain chipped teacup.

"Arthur, what is it?" Watson asked. "You look a bit sick. Are you a bit sick?"

Arthur swung his legs off the headboard, pivoted on his back, his brain chemicals so busy that he couldn't form words.

"Hello?" Watson said. "Do we need to talk this over?"

Arthur bounced from the bed, stood up.

Last night at the Prairie Dog Stomp, Mom had told the thief—the thief!—that he was investigating. That was, he calculated, a little more than twelve hours before. What was the thief doing now? If the thief knew that Arthur knew, that Arthur might go to the police, then the thief would be feeling desperate.

Arthur's heart began to pound; he realized he was scared.

"I gotta go," Arthur told Watson. "Catch ya later."

Watson said, "Poor choice of words, Arthur," but by then Arthur was halfway to the kitchen.

"Mom—" he began when he walked in, but instead he found Ramona, coloring at the table.

"In the shower," Ramona said. "What's up? Your face is funny."

"Not as funny as yours," Arthur said. "And I know who stole the necklace."

"Tell me!" Ramona said.

Arthur opened his mouth to speak but closed it again. Outside they both heard footsteps on the stairs, and then—a second later—the kitchen door flew open.

CHAPTER FIFTY-FOUR

t was Mrs. Merdle.

And right behind her was Grandpa, out of breath.

"Now, Amy," he gasped. "There is really . . . no need to go . . . barging—"

Mrs. Merdle was not ordinarily scary, but now she wore the same intense expression, eyes glittering, she'd worn when she'd denied there was any such thing as a teacup.

That expression was scary.

Arthur's heart stuttered. His knees weakened. He wondered why he'd ever started this whole detecting thing anyway. Wasn't it just fine to be good at customer service—and only good at customer service? There were probably a ton of people who lived whole happy lives never detecting a single darned thing. Mrs. Merdle was a runner and in good shape. Rushing up the stairs had not winded her the way it had winded Grandpa. Sounding almost normal, she said,

"Good morning, Arthur. Oh, and Ramona, too—hello."

Arthur, as scared as he was, replied, "Good morning." Habit's a wonderful thing.

"What are you even doing here? Did you bring Edie?" Ramona asked. "Arthur was just about to tell me—"

"Mo!" Arthur stopped her.

Mrs. Merdle pounced. "Tell you what?"

Ramona seemed to get that something was strange and didn't answer. Instead she looked from Mrs. Merdle to Arthur and said, "Uh . . . nothing. But, Grandpa, since you're here, we have some questions about that movie last night."

"Roger that, Ramona, but not just now," Grandpa said. Then he looked at Mrs. Merdle. "Since you've come this far, Amy, why not say your piece? And then you and I will adjourn downstairs, maybe get in touch with Len Bernstein. These kids can get back to enjoying their Sunday morning."

"It's your theory too, Byron," Mrs. Merdle said. "I don't get all the credit."

"Have it your way," Grandpa said. "But I never suggested we march up here like an invading army."

Arthur's heart had settled down, and he felt steadier

on his legs. It looked like detecting wasn't just detecting. There was another part too, and this was it, and you had to be a little brave—brave enough to face the bad guy.

Along with Mo and Grandpa, he waited.

"It grieves me no end to have to tell you this, Arthur." Mrs. Merdle put her hand to her heart, looked at her toes, took a long breath. "But I have come to the conclusion that Maria's friend Juan is in fact the person who stole your grandmother's necklace. Oh—and all the other jewelry, too."

Grandpa nodded. "Same as I said in the first place," he said with satisfaction. But then his formidable eyebrows collided in a frown, and he looked at Mrs. Merdle. "What other jewelry?"

Arthur had listened to enough Sherlock Holmes stories to recognize the detective's big moment, and he was going to get this right. He took a breath, wiped the bangs out of his eyes, looked directly at Mrs. Merdle, and spoke carefully: "Only two people know about the other stolen jewelry, Mrs. Merdle. One is me. And the other is the thief."

CHAPTER FIFTY-FIVE

After that, Ramona piped up, "Did you steal the teacup, too?" And then things got crazy.

Grandpa B turned on Mrs. Merdle. "Thief!" he hollered.

Mrs. Merdle skedaddled.

Fit as she was, she didn't get far.

Coming in to work, Jennifer Y happened to be crossing the parking lot, and Grandpa yelled: "Catch that woman!" and Jennifer Y did, grabbed Mrs. Merdle around the waist and held her.

Officer Bernstein arrived soon after that. Arthur expected him to handcuff Mrs. Merdle and haul her to jail. Arthur wasn't sure how he felt about that. Mrs. Merdle was a thief, but she was also Edie's grandmother and someone he'd known all his life.

The way it turned out, though, Officer Bernstein didn't handcuff her or haul her to jail. Instead he borrowed the office from Dad, talked to her for about an hour, made a deal for her to meet him at the BPD bright and early the next day.

Mrs. Merdle left without saying anything to anyone. Then Officer Bernstein called Arthur in to tell him what was what.

"I still don't have a report on the missing necklace," he explained. "And now I understand there's additional jewelry as well. We're going to need reports on each and every item. The paperwork will take time."

"What if she leaves town?" Arthur asked.

"Of course, I calculated the odds," Officer Bernstein said. "Ninety-seven to one against, based on local statistics for perps of her age and gender."

"Perps?" Arthur repeated.

"Perpetrators," Officer Bernstein said, "bad guys. And besides, she already confessed. Once she knew she'd been caught, she spilled the whole story. She also stole the Red File because her name was in it. And she stole that teacup back in the day—grabbed it when your grandma's back was turned. But I bet you knew that already."

Arthur nodded. "I did, but I don't know why."

"She just loved Jerry Strange and wanted to own

something that belonged to him," Officer Bernstein said.

"She believed what my grandpa had said? That Jerry Strange used to play tea party with it? But that story never made any sense," Arthur said.

Officer Bernstein nodded. "Exactly. It took her a long time, but when she figured it out, she returned the teacup to a shelf in the store."

Arthur shook his head. "That's crazy."

Officer Bernstein nodded sadly. "Yes, it is, Arthur. Would you say you have ever done anything crazy?"

Arthur thought of saying he'd organized a funeral for Ramona's pet mouse, that now the mouse's ghost lived in his room, that they were friends. Most people would call that crazy, wouldn't they? So he didn't say it. Instead he said, "Nothing that's illegal, I don't think. Nothing that's wrong."

"Good for you, Arthur," said Officer Bernstein. "I advise you to keep it that way."

Arthur and Officer Bernstein talked for a few more minutes. Before he left, Officer Bernstein clapped Arthur on the back and even came close to smiling. "Good job, my friend," he said. "You've solved the perfect crime."

• • •

That night Grandma and Grandpa came to dinner. So did Veda. They got pizza, the good kind from Locale, and ate at the kitchen table. Feeling bad about how he'd accused Juan of being a thief, Grandpa apologized to Veda and even paid for the pizza.

Veda didn't say "That's okay" or "Don't worry about it" or "We all make mistakes." But she nodded so Grandpa could see she had heard.

"Amy Merdle was always a terrible liar," Grandma said after Dad had served them all.

"'Terrible' as in she lied a lot?" Mom asked. "Or 'terrible' as in she was bad at it?"

"Both," Grandma said. "I remember one time she told us she was dating this guitarist, which was nonsense, and we all knew it. She was just envious of me 'cause I was with such a cute guy."

Ramona knitted her caterpillar brows. "What cute guy?" she asked.

"*Me*," Grandpa B said.

Ramona blinked, looked at Grandpa. "Really?" she said.

Grandma and Grandpa were sitting side by side at the kitchen table. Grandma looked affectionately at Grandpa B. "Yes, Ramona," she said. "Really."

Arthur hoped his grandparents were getting along better. When they were getting along, his grandpa was less crotchety.

"There are still a couple of things I don't understand," Mom said between bites. "And by the way, the pizza is delicious."

"Thanks. I made it myself," Grandpa said.

"Sometimes you're funny, Grandpa," Ramona said.

Mom looked from her daughter to her father. *"Sometimes,"* she said.

Arthur swallowed a big bite of the artichoke pizza, which was his favorite. "What do you want to know, Mom?" he asked.

"Well, I get it that Mrs. Merdle knew something only the thief would know," she said, "about the other jewelry being stolen, and I get that she was a suspect because she was in my book group—but I don't get how you narrowed that list down to her."

Leaving Watson out, Arthur explained. "So the saleswoman at Jumper Jewelers? When she saw Mrs. Merdle's earrings, she thought the prairie dogs were meerkats. And that made her think *Lion King.* I guess some, uh . . . people think Timon is the star of *The Lion King.*"

Veda's plate was empty. She sat back in her chair. "And

how did you know the necklace was at Jumper Jewelers at all?"

"I remembered the story Randolph told me about the ring he bought at the yard sale," Arthur said. "When Universal was closed, he went to Jumper to consign it."

Dad swallowed a bite, shook his head. "I still can't believe it. Mrs. Merdle was here a lot since she was moving and getting rid of stuff, downsizing. It sure never occurred to me that anything she brought us might be stolen."

Veda said, "Because she's a white lady?"

Arthur was shocked. Dad and Mom protested. Grandma frowned and shook her head.

Grandpa was the one who spoke up: "Oh, give the girl a break. You know, Veda, I've always liked you."

Veda looked at Grandpa, and Arthur could see that she felt nervous but wasn't going to back down. "I do know that," she said, and her voice shook a little. But when she looked at Arthur's dad and spoke again, her voice was steady. "No offense, Mr. Popper, but you didn't wonder if something was funny when Mrs. Merdle asked for her name to be kept in the Red File?"

Dad took a breath before answering. "Some people are funny about selling their stuff. They don't want the world to know. I just figured she was one of those people. I don't think it was because she was white? But maybe I should think about that." He shrugged, and the mood around the table relaxed a little.

Veda continued, "I get that she was clever to steal jewelry people didn't ever wear, but it still seems like she took a big risk. She should've expected someone would recognize their own jewelry in the case."

"Not necessarily," Grandma said. "Amy knew most of the women in my book group are too snobby to shop at Universal Trash, or they used to be. Since they didn't shop in the store, they'd never see their jewelry. Then Ramona here came up with that brilliant ad campaign, and now everyone shops at the store because everyone wants to save the planet."

Ramona wagged her thumbs at herself. "I am brilliant. So true," she said. Everyone laughed.

Arthur held out his plate. "Can I have another piece, please? Olive this time."

Arthur's dad served him.

"What about you, Veda?" Grandpa asked. "More pizza?" He was being extra nice.

"Yes, please," Veda said.

Grandpa served her, gave back her plate. Veda took a bite, chewed thoughtfully. "One more thing," she said. "Mrs. Merdle had enough money, didn't she? What did she do with what she got for stealing?"

By this time Arthur felt stuffed. "I should have mentioned that already," he said, "because it's kind of funny. According to Officer Bernstein, she gave it all to the prairie dogs."

Ramona's brows rose and fell. "Like, cash or gift cards or what?"

Everyone laughed again—but Ramona looked confused.

"For habitat, I think," Mom said. "In other words, to buy land that won't be used for houses or farming, land that's safe for prairie dogs."

Dad grinned and shook his head. "It's a sign of the times, isn't it? Robin Hood stole from the rich and gave to the poor. Mrs. Merdle stole from the middle class and gave to the prairie dogs."

"Don't make light of prairie dogs, dear," Mom said. "You remember what happened when we had those stuffed prairie dogs at the store, that taxidermy piece. All those protesters?"

Grandma said, "Whatever happened to those anyway, Dan? Did you sell them online or what?"

"Selling seemed like a bad idea," Dad said, "so I put them away."

"Where away?" Mom asked.

"Top of our closet, behind my old ski boots," Dad said.

Mom looked startled. "Are you serious? I had no idea."

Dad stood up to clear plates. "I'm all ears if you have a better suggestion."

"Um, actually . . . I guess I don't," Mom said.

Arthur looked at Ramona. "I do."

After a pause Ramona grinned. "I can make the coffin."

CHAPTER FIFTY-SIX

That night at bedtime, Arthur told Watson what Veda had said about Dad thinking Mrs. Merdle wasn't a thief because she was white.

"What do you think about that, Arthur?" Watson asked.

"I don't know," Arthur said. "I mean, maybe that's part of it. And also she was someone my family knew and someone who had money."

Watson tugged her whiskers. "Maybe . . ." she said slowly, "your family wouldn't have known her and she wouldn't have had money if she weren't also white?"

"Do you think that's true?" Arthur asked.

"I don't know," Watson said. "I'm a mouse, remember."

Arthur lay back in the blood-to-brain position. "It seems like it might be true, though. It seems like I should do more thinking."

"There's something else you should do," Watson said. "Enjoy that glowing sense of accomplishment. You've earned it."

"Thanks, Watson," Arthur said. "I plan to."

But, same as with everything else about detecting, enjoying it wasn't so easy.

Monday was warm, and the air was hazy. Sitting outdoors at the usual lunch table, Arthur thought he might smell a trace of smoke. He opened his lunch box, got out his sandwich, and prepared to make an announcement. "Guys," he said to Zeke, Danh, and Ethan. "I solved a mystery over the weekend, identified a jewel thief for reals!"

Then he waited, hoping for heaps of praise.

Zeke, Danh, and Ethan were chewing.

At last Zeke said, "Oh yeah. Who?"

Arthur was going to answer but remembered that Edie was a first grader at their school. One of the guys might recognize the name, and word might get around, and Edie might be embarrassed.

Arthur knew all about embarrassing grandparents.

"No one you know," he said. "But the thief stole a lot of stuff—a watch and a necklace and earrings. Big bucks."

"Any blood?" Zeke asked.

"How about weapons?" Ethan asked.

"Hundreds of bucks?" Danh asked. "Or thousands?"

Arthur's hopes for praise faded. "No blood, no

weapon," he said. "I don't know how many bucks."

Zeke finished his sandwich, wiped his mouth with the back of his hand. Danh took a small bite of his apple and chewed thoroughly. Ethan crammed a cupcake into his mouth and said something that might've been, "Cool."

Then Zeke said, "Whatever happened to that teddy-bear teapot or whatever it was? The one for your dolly tea parties?"

"It was a tea*cup*," Arthur said.

"Worth big bucks, right? Like the jewelry?" Zeke said.

"Never mind," Arthur said. "I just wanted to tell you I did something good for once, but—"

"High-five, Arthur," said Ethan, and held up his hand. It was sticky with cupcake frosting, but Arthur high-fived anyway.

On Wednesday during library time, Arthur returned the King Arthur book, and Mrs. Danneberg asked how he liked it.

"I never read it, Mrs. Danneberg," he admitted. "I was pretty busy last week. For a fact, I solved a mystery."

"The mystery of why Arthur won't read anything new?" she asked.

"A *real* mystery," Arthur said. "Stolen jewels. Not that anybody cares."

Mrs. Danneberg did not seem to care either. "That's nice. But I do wish you'd read your library books. You should learn more about King Arthur."

Arthur said, "I did watch a movie about him," but as soon as he said it, he worried. There was blood and that inappropriate part, even though he hadn't seen it.

"Movie," Mrs. Danneberg repeated, her eyes ready to roll.

"I watched it with my grandfather." Arthur hoped that sounded family friendly. "It's called *Monty Python and the Holy Grail.*"

"Ha!" Mrs. Danneberg said. "I love that movie. Only, some parts I don't understand. The elderberries? Why are they an insult?"

Some good things did happen that week.

Like that same day—Wednesday—Arthur finally worked up the courage to tell Grandpa he had been unfair to Juan. Compared to confronting a jewel thief, it wasn't that hard.

They were in the office, just the two of them. Grandpa

scowled. "I already told Veda I like *her*. Are you calling me a bigot?"

Arthur avoided the question. Instead, he said, "It's wrong to, uh . . . *assume* that a person 'doesn't want to work' or whatever because they look this way or that way, and for sure not because their skin happens to be a certain color or their accent's different from yours. Those kinds of ideas are poison, Grandpa. They make the world a worse place."

Grandpa mumbled something Arthur didn't catch, and he never stopped scowling.

Later, though, Arthur found out from Veda that Grandpa had phoned Juan himself to offer him the job again. Juan had said he would think about it.

On Friday, after Officer Bernstein had visited all the book group members to take reports on stolen jewelry, Susana Malarky sent an email saying he was so nice and so smart that they should invite him to join book group too.

"It would be good for us to have a guy's point of view," she wrote. "And maybe we'd cheer him up a little."

That same day after school, Arthur worked a shift at the store. He helped a new dad find a stroller, a grad student find place mats "so even though İ can't cook, my friends will be impressed when they come over," and a mom-aged woman find a pair of jeans because she'd lost weight when she'd started working out.

The woman was super grateful. "My friends will never believe a kid helped me shop for jeans," she said. "You have a real knack for customer service."

Arthur thought, *So what?* But he said, "I appreciate the compliment," and handed her back her purchase. "Thank you for shopping at Universal Trash."

It was five minutes to closing when the woman left. Randolph and Jennifer Y had already gone home, and Dad was in the office, so Arthur did the walk-through and hung up the CLOSED signs.

For a fact, the store is a cool place, he thought, looking around—the space, the colors, the shapes.

The awesome array of stuff.

He read Grandpa's words, posted by the door:

Herein the collected work of humankind
Some of it useful
Much of it useless
All of it for sale

Arthur's grandparents had built something that now belonged to his dad and mom, that supported their family.

And maybe Ramona was right. Maybe they really were saving the earth.

If the store became Arthur's someday, would that be so bad? Not to mention, you got way more praise for customer service than you ever did for detecting—and detecting was so much harder.

CHAPTER FIFTY-SEVEN

Arthur and Ramona set the time for the prairie dog funeral as two p.m. on Saturday. By 1:55, eight mourners had gathered in the parking lot—Mom, Dad, Grandma, Grandpa, Officer Bernstein, Veda, Arthur, and Ramona.

Randolph had been invited but had said no when he'd found out Officer Bernstein would be there.

Jennifer Y was covering the store.

Everyone had dressed nicely. Dad was wearing his Christmas tie with the squirrels on it. Mom was wearing Grandma's pearl necklace, which Officer Bernstein had returned that morning. Officer Bernstein himself was wearing his dress uniform.

"What do we do now?" Veda asked. "I've never been to a funeral before."

"I've been to too many funerals," Grandma said, "but never one quite like this."

Arthur said, "Just follow directions."

Ramona nodded. "We've got this."

Dad had removed the two stuffed prairie dogs from storage, had dusted their fur and polished all four eyes. That morning when it had still been cool, he and Arthur had come outside and dug a good-size grave beside Mouse 4's.

"Ready?" Arthur asked Ramona. No one had argued when she'd volunteered to go first, carrying the coffin. For decoration she had made a collage of landscape pictures from magazines. For wild animals, that seemed more appropriate than paint and glitter.

"Ready," she said.

Arthur pressed play. A guitar strummed; thin voices sang in harmony. Instead of "Let It Go," Grandma had recommended a HoneyJams song called "Truckin' on Up." Processing at flower-girl pace across the parking lot, his grandparents rocked out—but only a little. It was a solemn occasion.

"Dearly beloved," Arthur began when at last they stood by the grave. "We are gathered here today to say goodbye to two prairie dogs. We don't know a lot about how they lived or how they died. We don't even know if they had names. But prairie dogs, like all living things, deserve to be treated with respect. That is why we remember them today."

Veda had helped Arthur write this speech. He had wanted to call the prairie dogs "nameless," but Veda had pointed out that prairie dogs communicate, and for all she and Arthur knew, these two did have names—only, they were pronounced in prairie dog language.

Veda was right, and Arthur had changed the words.

"And now, Ramona," Arthur continued, "will you lay the dear departed to rest, please?"

Ramona nodded, knelt, set the coffin into the hole.

"Fare thee well now, prairie dogs," Arthur concluded. "Amen."

"Fare thee well. Amen," the other mourners said.

And that was the end of the prairie dogs. Or so everyone thought . . .

. . . till the ghost of one of them—Yip, her name was— showed up in Ramona's room that night.

Ramona didn't tell her mom or dad. But the next day she told Arthur. Remembering the time she had caught him talking to someone named Watson, she suspected he would understand.

Arthur had accepted Watson's appearance as natural magic—like an iris opening or a brilliant sunrise. When Ramona told him about Yip, though, he started to wonder. Did every rodent come back from the dead, and if they did, where were they all, and if rodents turned into ghosts, what about people?

He added these to the other questions banging around in his head. Like could a person like Grandpa get over old prejudices? Would Grandma forgive Mrs. Merdle? How about Randolph and Officer Bernstein?

Most important, was the glowing sense of accomplishment you got from detecting worth all the blood-to-brain effort?

Meanwhile, Ramona had questions for Arthur. "Do you think Yip knows the future? Is she here to fix my big problems?"

Arthur didn't think first graders had big problems. But he didn't say that. Instead he said, "You have to ask Yip. Why does she say she's here?"

Mo frowned and her caterpillar brows made a *V*. "To teach me. But that can't be right. I know plenty already. More than a prairie dog for sure."

Arthur laughed, which made Mo frown harder. "Oh,

fine," she said. "So in that case, what has Watson taught *you*?"

Arthur wiped the bangs out of his eyes. Maybe he should let his mom cut them after all. Sometimes they got in his way.

"Watson's a mystery," he said at last, "just like Yip. So that's made me realize how many mysteries are out there—in the universe, I mean. Besides that, she kept at me till I figured it out about the teacup. So I guess what she's taught me, the main thing, is that it takes hard work, but sometimes mysteries can be solved."

ACKNOWLEDGMENTS

All my books derive from a little o' this, a little o' that, mixed to form a story. In that, they are like life itself, except that life does not necessarily cohere, while a story is supposed to. In this case, the story began with two things: a really amazing junk store in northern Arizona where I took some items for consignment, and a story I heard about a Colorado official whose parents started a crazy-successful business selling wares at Grateful Dead shows back in the day.

To those elements I added my own fondness for a teacup that belonged to my late grandmother, my experience as a member of multiple book groups over the years, and a little magic, because magic always helps.

I wrote most of this book while I lived in Boulder, Colorado, surely one of the prettiest small cities in the world with some of the healthiest and most prosperous residents. There I was privileged to belong to the Rocky Mountain Chapter of the Society of Children's Book Writers and Illustrators (SCBWI), whose members remain an inspiration.

My mother died during the writing of this book, and I

suspect the presence of helpful ghosts in it may owe something to the presence of her helpful spirit in my life.

Besides my family, I'd like to thank my hard-working agent, Jennifer Mattson; my editor, Paula Wiseman; and the really excellent copyeditor Bara MacNeill, who astutely caught several potentially embarrassing mistakes. Just one example: I called paragliding *parasailing*—totally different things and something I, as a Boulder resident, should have known. Thank you, Bara! If there are remaining errors, they, for sure, are my own.

Finally, *Trashed!* is dedicated to some of the best neighbors ever, the Pearsall-Christman family: Zach, Hamil, Arthur, and Simon. Any resemblance between the real Arthur and the main character of this story may or may not be accidental.